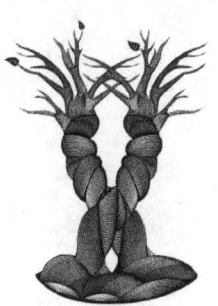

This book is a work of fiction. All characters in this collection are fictitious. Any resemblance to actual events or locales or persons, living or dead, is entirely coincidental.

Ayahuasca logo by Victoria Paul

ISBN-10: 0692531440
ISBN-13: 978-0-692-53144-0

STATES OF
TERROR
VOL 2

MATT E. LEWIS
KEITH MCCLEARY
EDITORS

ADAM MILLER
ART DIRECTOR

RYAN BRADFORD
JIM RULAND
ZACK WENTZ
CONSULTING ADVISORS

AYAHUASCA PUBLISHING
3245 UNIVERSITY AVE, STE. 1430
SAN DIEGO, CA 92104
AYAHUASCAPUBLISHING.COM

cover art by Adam Miller
table of contents art by Haig Demarjian

FOREWORD

In college I studied film, which would've been great, only I did it at Harvard, and they were strange about things. I don't think they were really comfortable with the idea of letting students actually *make stuff* as part of a degree program. So mostly we wrote a whole lot of papers about "the built environment" and "the gaze" and learned to say "signified" and "signifier" a lot. Which was fun! But what filmmaking there was, was mostly documentary. I don't even remember them having any lights.

On the other hand, what they *did* have—way down in the basement of the English department building—was an amazing old Oxberry animation camera. It was huge and creaky and took up an entire room and I rapidly found myself in love with it. I'd sit in my room, drawing thousands of little pictures, and then go in and shoot them for hours and hours, 24 drawings for every second of film, to make these weird little existential-type cartoons.

I remember when senior year rolled around, I had to go in to pitch the department my thesis project idea. I spent weeks working it out, storyboarding the whole thing on index cards, and then went in to present it to the departmental review board.

My thesis was a cartoon about Bigfoot and the Loch Ness Monster, to be done in the style of the *In Search of...* TV show. Bigfoot and Nessie were going to travel the globe, checking in with their other cryptozoological friends in order to perhaps finally solve the age-old question: *Do Human Beings Really Exist?*

I remember sitting there, flipping through my index cards, holding up one little scrawled doodle of a crazy monster after another to this very seriously professorial review board. I think it was somewhere around the Jersey Devil's soliloquy that I realized that they were looking at me oddly.

"But what's your thesis here? What are you trying to *prove*?" is the line that most echoes in my mind.

"Prove?" I remember thinking, as I stared at the floor.

"I just want to make a cartoon," I said.

Anyway, yeah, my thesis got turned down. It was humiliating—these people just don't understand! But, in the end, somehow, I graduated anyway, and eventually (except for some nights at 3 a.m.) forgot about the whole thing.

That is, of course, until I was asked to write this foreword, and—page by page—the whole thing came back.

Dammit, I kept saying, as I read through these stories, they should've let me do my cartoon! It would've been great!

But then I started thinking—it actually turned out okay. In that time senior year when I wasn't doing my thesis, I signed up to take some creative writing classes. I'd never done that before, and I found I was pretty good at it! That eventually led me to a career in screenwriting, and from there, eventually, to writing short stories—more than a few of which were about different kinds of monsters, and which, as a whole, led to me writing this foreword.

I know what you're saying: WHOA DUDE.

But it's true: sometimes it's the things that don't or can't exist that end up changing the course of your life.

Enjoy the book.

—*Ben Loory*

THE SOUTH

LOUISIANA ⬕ THE ROUGAROU

His Life in Glimpses of the Beast

KENTUCKY ◄ HOPSKINVILLE GOBLINS

Celestial Bodies; Bodies Terrestrial

FLORIDA ⬓ THE SKUNK APE

Welcome to Hell's Bay

WEST VIRGINIA ⬖ MOTHMAN

Friends With the Moon

NORTH TEXAS ⬗ LA LECHUZA

Wings, Bones

NORTH CAROLINA ◄ BEAST OF BLADENBORO

Beast Tours

ALABAMA ▮ THE WOLF-WOMAN OF MOBILE

Different Monsters

His Life in Glimpses of the Beast

Adrian Van Young

"When dealing with the devilish loup garou *Dupré urges caution, for the Cajun werewolf is capable of changing himself into any form at will."*

- Barbara Sillery, *The Haunting of Louisiana*

His people are from Lafayette but he is born in New Orleans.

Comes up only just in Treme, 7th Ward. Mother cleans the Roosevelt. Father drives the trolley cars. Has his formula cut with the foul Parish water. One brother at home. And the other three: gone. Two at Angola, the third OPP. Sister serves drinks on a gambling boat to men from other southern states.

Meditative, clear-eyed boy with freckles descending the bridge of his nose.

Hears brass instruments in the stifling dark. Mourning calls of river steamers. Walking home from the park watches streetlights wink out along Esplanade Avenue down from the arch.

The worsening of streets leads here: his mustard-colored shotgun house.

Comes up only just, by the scruff of his neck. Delicacy to the neighborhood bullies. Gets beat down all the time in school.

Father tells him: "Learn to fight." Then chuckles low. "Or learn to duck."

10 years old: his father goes.

Decides he will never speak to him again but two decades will prove him wrong.

In school and in its after-hours develops a fondness for stories of blood. Begins with Edgar Allan Poe. The wily hair, the dour cravat. Terror in the sunken eyes. Moves to

Lovecraft, Maupassant. Imagines the boys who gut-punch him at play, who twist his nipples and his hair, in elaborate schemata of pain and digestion. Sliced open by pendulums. Eaten by rats. Driven insane by unspeakable beings.

Brother who is still at home falls in with local troublemakers. Does petty crimes that seem like dares, that do not seem like crimes at all. Mark with this spray-can that falling down building. Pounce at that woman from this alleyway and cop that country ass, ya heard. Step in front of that tourist with this Louisville and ask him if he carries cash.

Is not—will never be—his brother. Hangs back in the shadows, hands clenched at sides.

Gets beat down less and less in school.

Finds letters in his brother's room from the other three brothers before him, in prison. One informs him: "Ain't got nothing you don't take it for yourself."

The year he is due to begin in high school they raze the oaks on North Claiborne and the city brings pylons and trucks of concrete to build the I-10 through the heart of his world. Businesses run by his neighbors shut down. A corridor of ruin forms. Shadows that favor his brother's routines and those of the boys that he runs with grow long.

First time he sees it is later that summer.

Are headed, the seven of them, him included, down Esplanade's neutral ground, walking their bikes. Ahead of them a lone female. Health worker, by the look of her.

It is almost midnight on a Tuesday in June and the woman is walking home after her shift.

It's there before what happens next.

Standing in the shadow of the half-built interstate. The deeper shadow there. So pale. The steel and concrete of the new overpass like the bones of some lizard god frozen mid-stride and there, underneath it, a thing he can't name. Not standing exactly but dangling upright. Dangling in the darkness like a sort of marionette. The limbs of a man. But the head of a beast. Wolf or a rabbit, he can't quite be certain and doesn't get to look again because that's when a series of gunshots explode.

One, two, three. A beat. Then four.

Health worker lies on the neutral ground, moaning. Part of her face torn away at the cheek.

Watches his brother, his brother alone, with the five other local boys working their bikes as they plummet down Esplanade under the oaks, the dark and the agonized oaks, up above them. Brother's face charging forward. His eyes in the dark. His mouth, which dangles slackly open.

A couple months later, the brother arrested along with several others for the murder of the woman. Truth of what happened emerges piecemeal.

Woman is a social worker. Clinic out in Metaire. Has a crusty old white man as one of her patients who molested a couple of kids years ago and now this social worker knows. When she says she will tell the authorities on him, old man doubles down and takes matters in hand.

Hires a contract on her life in the bad neighborhood that she walks through for work. Every night at 1 a.m. Takes the bus to the streetcar again to the bus and she walks through the neighborhood six days a week.

His brother is one of the neighborhood boys the white man approaches to put in the work.

Sentence: life without parole. The longest charge of all the brothers.

But all he can think of: the dangling thing. So pale, with the head of a rabbit or wolf.

After his brother goes down, he shapes up. Cuts ties with other wayward boys. Is not one, he knows. Had been lonely is all. Befriends other not-ones. Is lonely no more.

Does well in school. Supremely well. Has a knack for the intrigue and bloodshed of history. Works a counter: PO' BOYS/SAUSAGE/BLACKENED CATFISH/GRITS/GULF SHRIMP. Puts a little money by. Goes to the movies alone when it suits him. In the dark of the movie house thinks of his brother. His murderer's face charging under the oaks.

Never forgets the dangling thing though learns to think about it less.

A myth from his boyhood resolves into focus. Someone or other, his grandmother, maybe, had told him about it on brisk autumn nights. The rumoroo? The ruggleroo?

The Rougarou, he thinks. Of course.

The Rumoroo would make sense, too, for he knows there have only been rumors about it. Cajun werewolf on the loose in swamp country near Lafayette. A thing that looked like you or me with the head of what looked like a wolf or a rabbit among the marsh grass and the gaunt cypress knees, its shadow forever a few feet before it.

Rougarou will suck your blood. Rougarou will eat your flesh. Get your blood sucked or your flesh gobbled up, behold, the Rougarou is you. Even look at one, some say, the curse will take up in your eyes. Everywhere a Rougarou and Rougarou is where you're at.

Last few years in New Orleans remains inside on Mardi Gras. When mother and sister ask what is the matter tells them that he likes the calm. The feeling of being suspended in stillness when nobody breathing can seem to slow down.

McDonogh 35 with honors. Morehouse on scholarship. Sprawl of Atlanta.

Declares early major in History. Drinks liquor. Staggers through the darkened streets. Goes to decorous functions with Spelman U girls that seem to embody the phrase twice as good.

Sophomore year his mom sends word that his murderer brother has been killed in prison. His face in the dark charging under the oaks is painfully sharp for a week.

But it fades.

And then a stark coincidence. The oldest one has been released and has moved back to Kerlerec Street with their mother. Concedes that God works in mysterious ways. Resolves he will visit the first chance he gets.

Reads books. Ancient Egypt: Osiris. Anubis. Bronze Ages—early, middle, late. Meets a girl named Shaundraneka the summer before his senior year. Spelman girl from Mississippi. Big natural hair with the slenderest neck.

All that fall they spend in bed.

Forgets about the Rougarou all through the spring of that same year.

One night in the week before their graduation, driving home from Shaundra's dorm, is on 29 N when he makes a lane change without putting his blinker on. Eruption of lights from a Georgia State Trooper. Swerves behind his Pontiac: dented muffler, flaking teal. Initiates the traffic stop. His heart is slamming in his chest. Why he hadn't caught sight of car's dome of lights like the fin of a shark cutting through open water for many years after that night he can't concretely say.

Slows down.

That's when he gropes in the pants he is wearing only to find that his wallet is missing. Has left it back in Shaundra's room where they had paid for take-out with it, too wrapped up in each other's heat to pick up their clothing and eat in the commons.

Is not a stranger to the cops. Has dealt with them in New Orleans. They are so rotten there, he thinks, that they will be creamsicles here in Atlanta.

Cop is round and raw-faced like a skinless tomato.

Yessirs, nossirs expertly until the matter of the license.

The violation happens fast. One moment he is in the car, the next one bent over the hood wearing handcuffs. Thinks: *It is finally happening to me.* Says over his shoulder: "I see your badge number."

Policeman wrenches him around and billy-clubs him in the eye.

Feels the eye swell in his head and explode. Finger-shade of red descends. Other eye is blinking fiercely, protective of the world it knows. Feels himself being rotated again as the orbital blood gushes over his shirt and when he is bent again over the hood, through his remaining eye, it's there.

Beyond the guardrail. In the dark. The dangling wolf-headed or rabbit-eared thing like a birthday show puppet unevenly stitched from the sugar-high carnage of disparate puppets and sees in what light from the night-lamps there is that its body is hairless and sheer and moon-white.

"Hold still, nigger," says the cop.

Is no longer, however, struggling. Doesn't even feel the pain. Sees only the Rougarou waiting in shadow at the place where freeway embankment descends, harbinger or avatar he cannot at the moment say.

Something is wrong with the Rougarou's jaw. A jaw should never hinge like that. Unlatching toward him so, so wide that the chin is on a level with the bottom of the belly and no teeth inside it, just darkness unyielding, enclosed by the white borderlands of the mouth.

Taut on its hind-legs. Its paws crooked before it.

Trying to make out its eyes, passes out.

A night and a day and a night in the tank. Paper-towel poultice scotch-taped to his eye. Only gets out when Shaundra's father shows up, makes much of a brother in Jackson PD.

A couple days before he walks to receive his diploma in Near Eastern Studies, ophthalmologist says he is blind in one eye.

When he crosses the stage, Provost seizes his hand. His gauze with its crust of brown matter is hot on the graduate stage in the Georgia May heat. Clasps his shoulder. Photo Op.

Whispers to him: "We were kings."

Marries Shaundra. Life goes on.

Couple makes plans to remain in Atlanta. Craftsman house in Decatur. Other Negroes with values. Lectures at Morehouse and Spelman in history. Shaundra works at a bank. Mortgage down on the house. Make a baby their second year out.

It miscarries.

Expects to see the Rougarou but the walls of their craftsman are silent and dark.

Agree that Atlanta is bad juju for them. Relocate to New Orleans. As soon as they make the decision to go, Shaundra finds out she is pregnant again. Ascribe this luck to where they're headed: city of balconies, city of waters.

At thirty: long-muscled, light-skinned and broad-shouldered. Freckles now faint on the bridge of his nose. Instead of an eye wears a black pirate patch that Shaundra says is regal on him. Voice is low and statesman-like but is higher when he has had wine or is lying.

Baby comes. A silk-soft girl.

They name her Beth Anne after Shaundra's grandmother.

Neighbor is a young trombonist who wakes up Beth Anne from her afternoon naps. Drummer lives across the street. The town is full of music, music, he cannot believe he'd forgotten how much. One day means to storm next door to command the trombonist to stop for an hour but the music, aloose in the air of the street, unmuffled at last by the wall that they share, is so lovely and sad that he pauses mid-knock.

Listens through the final note.

At the local CC, picks up history courses that land him in a full-time job. Shaundra gets in on the buzzing ground floor of a new credit union, associate-status.

Tender wrinkles on the bottom of his baby daughter's foot, glowing in the morning sun.

Clicking through slides of the pharaohs and gods, goes faster a half-click explaining Anubis. Protector of the sacred dead. Overseer of bleedings and mummifications. The form of a man with the head of a jackal. The virile and sinister ears. The black snout.

Resumes ties with his mother, in middling health. His sister, moved on from the gambling boat circuit, tending bar in the Marigny three nights a week. Paroled from Angola his oldest big brother, who is hot on sobriety, God, work-release.

His brother is also a husband, a father. Also loves slasher movies and heavy brass music. *The blood is strong*, he almost thinks, but banishes the sentiment as somehow beneath him.

Almost asks him has he seen it: the thing with the head of a rabbit or wolf.

But how can he open himself to someone, he decides in the end, who has squandered a life?

His father returns. All these years unaccounted. The ex-trolleyman with the strangler's hands. Has been to places—New York City, Baja California, El Paso, Slidell. When asked for the reason why he went away, father says it was him and his four older brothers, how they were dropping one by one. He could not stand to see them all. How it spoke to his failure, he says, as a father, that they had not been better men, never thinking for a moment that the fact of his absence had been meaningful on that score in the least.

Grows closer to him in a meaningless way. 7th Ward bars, second-lines and cookouts. Sometimes on Sundays at St. Augustine's but not without long afternoons at the track where you can catch Allen Toussaint, his father says, if you are looking. Discovers that he likes to drink in a way that is different from drinking in college.

Teaching his classes begins to grind on him. Over-enrollment, department committees. His students work two, sometimes even three jobs. Marriage to Shaundra starts showing its seams. Mistakes her affection for wanting to own him.

Finds being a father to Beth Anne is hard. Girl is always, aggrievedly, catching him at it.

Shaundra says the new distance is due to his father. A man he owes all but a kick in the ribs. But he acts out against her. Gets cruel and defensive, even when he knows she's right.

Or wants badly to think he knows.

Sleeps in the living room. Sleeps in his office. A go-cup is never not crushed in his hand. Still imagines his life to be basically good in spite of the fact that he won't let it be.

Only when Shaundra suggests it to him admits that he may be depressed.

They leave Beth Anne with Shaundra's sister. Travel out to a cottage in old Cajun country a few miles west of Lafayette. It is at his mother's advice that they go.

Digging under the demon that keeps them apart.

Breaux Bridge gives them oysters. They motor the swamp. The basin of Atchafalaya at dawn.

Attempt to make love in the cottage that night but give up when he can't get hard.

Last morning they go to the breakfast buffet. The menu is boudin and eggs. Eating their breakfast and drinking their coffee while the French tourists next to them plot out their day when he sees there among the old Mardi Gras photos and among the group portraits of checked fishing parties a hideous series of minstrelsy masks arrayed along the café wall. The one in the middle, the Al Jolson face. Stamped on the forehead a single word: "Darkie."

She says, "If you love me, then you will complain."

"They'll laugh our asses out the door."

"We. Are. Paying. Customers. You don't say something, I will."

But he doesn't say anything. Sidetracked by something. Corner of the window from the corner of his eye, his one good eye: a loose-limbed shape. There, in the marsh grass behind the café. A dithering finger of manicured swamp to impress on the tourists they're in savage country and that's where he sees it, the dangling thing, and knows when he does that his marriage is over.

Ignores Shaundra's curses. Gets up from the table. Wanders down among the trees.

Rougarou stands on the opposite bank. Obscured but for its neck and head. Watching him over the murk of the swamp, its jaw swaying open in plain light of day.

Crashes into the swamp to attract or pursue it, his mouth coffee-acrid, his gut full of sausage. Takes off loping. Hounded thing. Keeps behind the screen of trees. It is so tall, its strides so big that even when hidden it humps into view. Its slinking armature is white and its hackles move over its head as it runs and the jaw swings before it, a bowl on a swivel.

In panting despair at the edge of the swamp, he holds his hand against his mouth.

The shadow of the Rougarou projects both behind and before it in time and the worst thing he about it, he figures, is this: he can never approach it. Can never catch up.

His life deserts him piece by piece.

Job at community college dissolves. Loses faith in Antiquity's great sand-blown dramas. Draws deeper and deeper inside of himself.

Shaundraneka kicks him out.

Single-occupancy on Elysian Fields. At the local Head-Start, teaches world history classes. Gets comped heavy pours at the neighborhood dive where his sister no longer looks over the bar.

Shambles down Decatur nights. The Mississippi's rushing hide. Lumbering man in the raggedy sweatpants. Patch that hides his ruined eye. Six-pack of Abita, his bumbling claw, betrays the fact that he is near.

Keeps his head lowered but comes to a point, in the hoary and drunken extreme of his evening, when he cannot say where he goes. If he is really there at all. And so, to mark the deficit, makes wild campaigns against the night.

Kicks a cat to see it screech.

Breaks his bottles on the levee with a gritting of his teeth.

Comes upon lovers who neck on the banks and moves on them with gangling limbs.

Checks in with Beth Anne on the weekends. Is awkward. Is cautiously furtive, not wanting to be. Wants this to be their special time, though often as not he is badly hungover. When one day going through the zoo it's there behind a pane of glass: the Rougarou for Mardi Gras. A humanoid wolf rearing up on its haunches. Human skulls about its feet. Its chop-swaying, cartoonish jaws. Topaz beads around its neck. Patched out of purple, green and gold, a jester's hat with silver bells.

In the glare of the statue's enclosure, his face.

"Daddy?" says Beth Anne. "You there?"

Celestial Bodies;
Bodies Terrestrial

Danielle Renino

"A creature with its arms stretched high was approaching: it was three or three and a half feet tall, with large round eyes on each side of its head that glowed yellow; the being itself shone silver, as if lighted from within; its head was bald and egg-shaped, narrowing to a pointed chin, with a horizontal slit for a mouth, a conical nose tapering to a point with a ball on the end of it, and enormous 'elephant-like' ears. Its body was thin, with an oversized muscular looking upper torso and arms so long they practically dragged on the ground, with long taloned hands. . . two antennae on top of the head."

- Bruce Rux, *Architects of the Underworld*

It's August again and the leaves are dry, the farm is quiet. August and Daddy's having trouble sleeping. His shotgun is never far from his side. He doesn't let me out after dark. August and I sit by my window, running my fingers along the tiny square hole in the corner of my screen. A memento from the year before. August and humming can be heard at night, out over the trees, where the stars boil and burn, and I know it's only a matter of time.

August in Christian County, Kentucky.

I open my screen, stick my head out the window, and look to the sky.

Look for the lights.

⬤

Sometimes in the afternoons I sit next to the spot where we torched the body. Back in the cornfield, between the rows of rustling green. Our crop grows ten feet high, miles of chattering corn, and stuttering leaves. Along the outskirts of the field the wind works its way through the rows, it bends the stalks and their movement sounds like singing, but not here. There is no singing here. This place is sullied.

The creature's grave is a clearing about five feet in diameter, marked by dried grass and the blackened remnants of the timber that we used for kindling. We weren't sure if it would burn. Daddy lit the match and I watched from within the stalks, the tall corn reaching out to cradle me softly to its chest. The smoke wafted up over the rows. It scarred the summer air. The creature began its slow descent to ashes, and Daddy turned to me and spoke above the hissing flames.

"Alexis, come here baby. There's nothing to be afraid of."

"It wasn't an angel," I said, and that's all I could say. It came from the sky, but it wasn't an angel. An angel cast down, perhaps. A monster of a different maker. A crack in our church's stained glass, a spot of blood on the white of my communion dress. There's no such thing as aliens...demons, goblins maybe, but not aliens.

"Baby, it's okay," Daddy said, and raised his hands to the sky. "*For I have given you power to tread serpents and scorpions underfoot, and to trample on all the power of the Enemy; and in no case shall anything do you harm.* So saith the Lord. Baby, in no case shall anything do you harm."

"In no case shall anything do me harm," I repeated back, though my voice wavered.

The air smelled like salt, young crop, and melting flesh. There's no such thing as aliens...

"Amen."

◢

We didn't kill it. Daddy tried, but no matter how many times he shot the thing, it refused to die. Every time he hit it, in the chest, in the arm, in one of its atrophied legs, the creature didn't so much as flinch. Every time a bullet ricocheted off its body, the sound was like stones hitting a metal pail. With force. With frustration. I still hear the sound sometimes, at night when things are too quiet and the harvest moon hangs weeping in the sky. When the lightning bugs speak Morse code in the distance, and I'm convinced the lights are back. The lights that brought the monsters.

Daddy was on his way back from town when the flickering started. It was eight o'clock. At first it was a soft swelling of the night sky. That's the best he could put it, "swelling," like an inflamed cut glowing red and raw. A loud hum could be heard over the rumble of our pick-up truck, an old rusted thing that was on its last legs. Daddy later told me that he drove the whole way home clutching the steering wheel so tight that his knuckles burned white, his foot rammed down on the accelerator. Daddy is tall and thin, but strong, and I remember my first reaction when he told me was surprise that he didn't break the car, that the accelerator didn't snap from the pressure. As he drove, he told me later, the lights grew more vicious and the swelling burst, like a hive of wasps kicked open. He was convinced they'd disappear before he got home.

They didn't.

"Alexis!" He called once he'd made it back to the farm, already halfway up the porch steps. "Alexis, get out here quick!"

I hurried out onto the porch, my damp hair half-braided. It was a messy cascade of chestnut curls that began to untangle as soon as I craned my neck to see what Daddy was yelling about. Bobby, a boy from my bible group had asked me out on a movie date, and I had been struggling with my hair for the last hour. Up, down, straightened, curled. I couldn't make up my mind.

"Daddy, what's wrong?" I asked, and he swept a hand towards the sky.

"You can see it clearly now," he said. "Before it was just a swelling. The sky was swelling, but now...look!"

Up over the trees, there was a revolving prism of color. Bleeding, sparking, sweeping in from some unseen source. The night sky lit up, a rainbow of flames, lightning the color of rose petals and exotic spices.

"What's going on?" I asked, my voice hushed. The brilliance of the lights bleached out the weak freckling of stars.

"Rapture," he said. "It's the Rapture."

The lights continued to flash for a few more seconds, zipping closer, bathing our cornfield in rays of wine and sanguine. Washing over the pig pen.

Our pigs squealed the way they do before Daddy butchers them, long stomach-churning screams. The spill of fear that comes with the end of days. And in that moment I believed. I could feel it in the air, the electricity, the madness. Something was coming.

The lights spread out over the farm.

And then they were gone.

Nine o'clock. Daddy and I sat in the living room. Daddy in his big blue recliner, me on the floral patterned couch. There was a tear in the corner of one of the cushions and I pulled at the stuffing that leaked out through the slit. Daddy poured over his Bible. I canceled my date with Bobby.

"Ah! Here it is, Alexis. *For as the lightning cometh forth from the east, and is seen even unto the west; so shall be the coming of the Son of man*," Daddy said with vigor. "Baby, we have seen the lightning."

"It wasn't really lightning, Daddy," I said, still pulling at the couch. "I'm not sure what it was..." It was *like* lightning, but the flashes of color were too drawn out. There wasn't enough violence or natural force to them. They reminded me more of airplane lights than lightning strikes. As it was, I was beginning to doubt Daddy's Rapture theory. An hour had passed and nothing else had happened.

Daddy opened to a new passage. "*And I looked, and, behold, a whirlwind came out of the north, a great cloud, and a fire enfolding itself, and a brightness about it, and out of the midst thereof as the color of amber, out of the midst of the fire*," he read, he offered as proof.

"It might have been an airplane," I said, even though I didn't believe it. I wasn't sure what I believed.

"Alexis, you gotta have faith." Daddy flipped the thin pages of the Bible, his strong hands threatening to tear the paper. "Listen to this. *Behold! I tell you a mystery. We shall not all sleep, but we shall all be changed, in a moment, in the twinkling of an eye, at the last trumpet. For the trumpet will sound, and the dead will be raised imperishable, and we shall be changed. For this perishable body must put on the imperishable, and this mortal body must put on immortality.*"

As Daddy spoke I heard a light thumping coming from upstairs. Thump, scrape, scrape, scrape; the sound of feet and claws. It reminded me of when a raccoon had gotten into the attic a few summers before, and we could hear it move panicked across the ceiling.

"Daddy, do you hear that?" I asked, but he was too busy quoting his passages, his voice thundering with conviction.

The noise continued, the grating sound of sharp nails and a warm body. At first I thought it was an animal, another raccoon or squirrel, stuck in the attic and trying to find its way out. Then the sound multiplied. Many feet. Many claws. Thumping. Scraping. Like a rain of stones. Closer and closer. From above. From below. Outside. All around. A rain storm, or a reaping.

And Daddy's voice above it all.

"Rejoice that your names are written in heaven. Rejoice, rejoice, rejoice."

"Daddy!" I cried and he stopped mid-sentence, his head turned towards the living room window.

"What in the..." He rose to his feet, the Bible falling from his lap.

There were creatures looking in the window at us. Not raccoons. Not squirrels.

Monsters. The size of small children, with large yellow eyes and pointed ears. Silver skin, that glistened when they moved, like they were slick with oil. They peered in the window, heads tilted to the side. Tapped at the glass with long, claw-like fingers. Silver, and silver, and silver. The yellow of their eyes was the only thing about them that didn't shine metallic.

Demons...but unlike any demon I had ever imagined. The fire in the sky had brought them, the light had cast them down. They had to be demons, the other possibility made no sense. There was no way. Creatures from the sky. I didn't dare think the name, it felt too blasphemous.

"*So God created mankind in his own image, in the image of God he created them; male and female, he created them,*" I whispered, my throat dry. "He created them..." But these things... they came from the sky. They're not from here...they were not created here...

Daddy grabbed two of his shotguns off the wall.

"Alexis," he said, his voice frenzied. "You remember that time we went hunting, right? You remember how you shot that pheasant?"

I nodded even though we took the trip when I was eleven, almost four years ago. Even though I remembered the trip, I couldn't rightfully say I remembered how to shoot.

"Just pretend this is pheasant hunting." He shoved one of the shotguns into my hands and headed for the door. "You stay up in your room. No matter what, you stay in your room until I call for you."

I hurried up the stairs and Daddy's shotgun sounded three times. Blast after blast, followed by cursing, followed by prayer.

I was up in my room for what felt like hours, my knees drawn up under my chin, the gun laid out at my feet, harsh against my pale peach bedspread. I waited for the shrill sound of Daddy's shotgun, the only sign I had that he was ok. And the metal ping, that I would learn later was the sound of the bullets bouncing off the creatures. I bent my head.

"Then God said, Let Us make man in Our image, according to Our likeness; and let them rule over the fish of the sea and over the birds of the sky and over the cattle and over all the earth, and over every creeping thing that creeps on the earth." I repeated it slowly, purposefully. There is nothing else out there. Only us. Only here. For God said...

I waited for a long time before I got up the courage to look out the window. I picked up the gun and wandered over, cautious steps that caused the floor to creak. Outside I could see Daddy chasing the creatures, waving his gun. The creatures floating back towards the forest, their legs twisted up underneath them.

"What the holy hell..." I whispered, and opened my window, pressed my nose up to the screen, trying to get a better look at the things. "But there's no such thing as-"

One of the creatures pressed it face up to the window.

I yelped, and jumped back.

I looked at it for a few moments. Up close its yellow eyes were mixed with darker shades of orange and gold. Wet eyes. Searching. I looked at it, and it looked back. Then, I aimed my gun towards the window, and pulled the trigger.

The night went on and on like this. The creatures advanced towards the house. Rounds of gun fire sounded. Prayer after prayer. The pigs thrashed and squealed. Until just after three in the morning, when it all stopped. The creatures disappeared. Back up into the sky...and as the sunrise leaked across the sky, I had to remind myself. There's no such thing as aliens.

The one we burned died on its own, after the others left. There were ten or twelve of them in total, and they either left it behind or it stayed on its own accord. I have nightmares sometimes and in these terrors it peers its face in my window, and rips at the bullet wound in corner of my screen, prying and prying until it finds its way in.

In the dreams I cry for Daddy, but no words come out, and the thing looks at me with slick eyes, the color of a bobcat's, hungry eyes.

I found it about a week after the incident, sprawled out between the rows, baking in the August sun. The smell it gave off was frightening, like old blueberries and something sour, something I couldn't name. The smell of sweetness and infection. There was a horsefly sitting on the thing's open eye, and the corn murmured secretly among itself.

I ran and told Daddy, and he put on his thick rubber gloves, and the rubber overalls he wears when he slaughters the pigs.

"We can't call the police, Alexis," Daddy told me, his hands planted firmly on my shoulders, the rubber rough against my skin. "You know what would happen."

"They wouldn't believe us," I answered solemnly.

"We gotta take care of this ourselves," Daddy said. "I'll get the matches."

It's August again and the lightning bugs sigh, and the farm hums. August and I spend too much time in the cornfield. Rows and rows of smoke scorched crop. August and I can't stop thinking about the creatures, with their small silver bodies, and claws the color of paring knives.

August and with my screen up, and my head out the window, I see them.

Lights, swollen red over the cornfield.

Welcome to Hell's Bay

Stephen T. Brophy

"If there's a conclusion to the Skunk Ape enigma, it would be that credible people, often professional people, have seen something that appeared to be a giant two-legged shaggy creature that stinks to high heaven."

- Charlie Carlson, *Weird Florida*

COMING 2019
THE VILLAGE AT HELL'S BAY
EXCLUSIVE FLY-IN COMMUNITY AND RESORT
A deMand Consortium Project

the sign read, or at least it used to. Now it was covered in something thick and damp that may have been mud, with holes punched through it like a shotgun blast, though there were no signs of buckshot. More like it had been pounded with rocks. Or very powerful fists.

Leland deMand observed the carnage from behind tinted glass as his limo rolled to the fringes of the swamp. Whatever had been at the machines had done a number on them. The windows of a backhoe's cab were smashed, its roof dented. A bulldozer's engine had been yanked out and strewn across the marsh, and an excavator had been tipped on its side like a bovine victim of drunken redneck tomfoolery.

Leland's teeth clenched around the unlit Cuban between his thick, wet lips, and he gagged on a small bite of hand-rolled tobacco that tumbled down his tongue. *The nerve*, he thought, his gray stare panning across the wreckage and over to the cluster of filthy, thrift store-shopping, sloganeering hippie wannabes chanting verbal diarrhea at the site's perimeter.

"Go to Hell, not Hell's Bay!" they chanted over and over. If they wanted a devil, he would show them one.

Burke, his driver and bodyguard, worked his enormous frame out of the driver's seat and came around to open Leland's door. Carmen laid a hand on Leland's shoulder.

"This will set us back a few days," she said.

She'd earned her position as his executive assistant by winning the fourth season of *Sell Yourself*, the reality competition show Leland produced and hosted. Her capacity to gently maneuver him, physically and emotionally, had all but clinched the deal. But that was three seasons ago, and the old tricks didn't work like they used to.

"The hell it will!" Leland barked, shaking free of her as he climbed out into the claustrophobic humidity of the swamp.

The chanting grew louder at the sight of him, accompanied by a backing chorus of hisses and boos. It was the kind of public disapproval that normally warmed Leland's heart.

"You people think you've accomplished something?!" he roared, his Boston accent betraying Southie roots. "Sure, you cost me time! You maybe even cost me money! But I got money comin' outta my ass! And I can buy all the goddamn time I need. I can make it move backwards, forwards or goddamn sideways! If I want, the Sun goes 'round the Earth or the Moon turns into a fuckin' strobe light! You losers have *no idea* what I can do! What I can make happen! Hell, I snap my fingers and *poof*, you all disappear! Forever! Ain't that so, Burke?"

Burke said nothing, just stood there with his arms crossed at the wrists, muscles bulging at the seams of his suit, eyes unreadable behind teardrop shades, bald head gleaming in the morning heat.

The chant shifted gears. "Leland deMand, get off our land!"

Leland laughed.

"*Your* land? This land was sold to me fair and square by the University of Florida, because apparently there's not enough educatable brains down here to justify them holdin' onto it. Lookin' at you pack of shitbags, I have no doubt that's fair reasoning. So whether you like it or not, this is happenin,' people, so either put in a bid on a lot, or get your asses gone!"

A blast of noise, wind and swamp spray filled the air as an airboat tore up the channel, slowing as it approached the job site. At the controls was a whippet-thin stretch of human scarecrow in scraps of flannel and denim, a filthy trucker hat pulled low over tanned leather flesh. As he hopped from the boat and sank his boots into the marsh mud, he spat thick brown juice between two teeth that reminded Leland of the goo covering his Under Construction sign.

"You the law?" Leland asked. "Because I want all these people arrested, and I'm not sure they're all gonna fit on that airboat."

"Can't help ya there," the swamp-man drawled. "Barnaby MacPherson. Most folks call me Scooter." He stuck out a hand that looked like it had an estranged relationship with soap and water and deMand nodded at Burke, who shook it on his behalf.

"So why're you here?" Leland asked.

"I'm here to offer my exper-tease. Now, if ya'll'll excuse me..."

Scooter commenced inspecting the area, examining the damaged vehicles, poking at debris, sniffing the air like a Bluetick Coonhound, even picking a sample of the brown slop from the sign. He brought it close to his eye and nose, then rolled it into a small ball between thumb and forefinger.

Leland, Burke and Carmen crossed the muddy field with him, following his trail from place to place.

"So, if you're not law enforcement, do you mind me asking what exactly you think it is you're doing?" Leland asked. "Because I don't see how this is helping."

"Right with ya," Scooter said, extracting a set of rusty tweezers from his shirt pocket and plucking a brownish-red clump of what appeared to be animal fur from a mangled edge of the overturned excavator. He held it up high in the morning sun and turned to the gathered activists.

"Ya'll out here protestin' the wrong thing, as usual," he said. "This ain't about no endangered crocodiles or tearin' up a hikin' trail. What we got here is a Skunk Ape."

The protesters erupted in laughter, a few emitting ecstatic whoops.

"A skunk what?" deMand asked, frowning hard enough to crease his Botoxed forehead.

"Only skunk ape I see is the one on your head, deMand!" one of the protest ringleaders shouted, gesturing to the elaborate swirl of bleached combover nesting atop Leland's balding dome.

This brought more laughter. He was tempted to unleash Burke on them, the only thing staying his hand the PR disaster that would follow.

"Skunk Ape, Mr. deMand," Scooter declaimed. "Humanoid hominid known to inhabit the Everglades region. No one knows exactly how many're left, but they're practically a protected species, or would be if they'd just pushed that damn bill through the legislature back in '77. Though from the looks of your job site, you're the species needs protectin'."

"Okay, I see," Leland said with icy calm. "You're insane."

"Could be," Scooter replied. "But I know what I know. I've had no less than a half dozen encounters with these critters in the last forty years, starting when I was just eleven. They can be mean and ornery, but mostly all they want is to be left alone."

"I'll keep that in mind," Leland said with a smirk that only grew smirkier when he caught sight of the sheriff's vehicles rolling into the clearing.

Disappointing as it was, Leland had to content himself with the protesters being chased off his property rather than the mass arrests he'd been angling for. While the cops understood what Leland was bringing to the table, they were locals sympathetic to the rights of the whiners, if not to their cause. Even the crackpot cryptozoologist was allowed to board his airboat and jet off into the mist rather than be remanded to the custody of a psychiatric facility for the good of himself and others. Chances are he was less insane than he was a shrewd small-timer, a man who'd latched onto his niche and found a way to game the system. Leland could almost admire that, but it was a squirmy kind of admiration mixed with an unwelcome sensation of pity.

"The downside is we know they'll be back," Leland said. Burke nodded, tensed up like a pitbull.

"So, we install a few cameras around the perimeter, hire a handful of nightwatchmen, and be ready for them," Carmen said. It was the kind of no-nonsense, easily enacted suggestion that had helped garner her *Sell Yourself* victory back in the day. Surely Leland would sign off on it quickly so they'd be able to get the hell out of this backwater and back to the Northeast.

"I don't think so," said Leland. "This operation is far too precious to be entrusted to a buncha contractors with no skin in the game. Guys like that, we go hire local, someone's liable to pay 'em off to fall asleep on the job. Hell, everyone down here is everyone else's second cousin. For all we know, we'd end up paying our own saboteurs."

Carmen frowned, but caught herself and willed a more neutral expression. She was much too young for worry lines. "So what? We leave Burke?"

Carmen couldn't tell if Burke was looking at her, past her, or straight into her soul behind those shades. She'd heard him speak so rarely, she couldn't even summon an idea of what his voice sounded like. In her more imaginative moments, she wondered if he wasn't some kind of high-end, next-gen cyborg. one of those expensive supertoys that only men in Leland's rarefied stratus could afford.

"Oh, Burke's staying alright," Leland said. "But he won't be alone. Afraid I can't pass the buck on this one."

"Are you saying...*you're* staying?"

Leland curdled his lips in what he probably thought was a devilish grin. "It's not unprecedented."

"Okay, well, I can arrange to have your private trailer delivered here on my way back to the hotel," Carmen said, pulling out her iPhone.

"Hotel?" Leland asked as he caught her wrist. "No need for that, dear. You're staying, too."

"Oh," she said, trying not to let her features distort into a mask of permanent disappointment.

❜

Leland's custom mobile home was a genuine land yacht that put most A-list actors' set accommodations to shame. It was three levels inside, with media room, kitchen and dining on the bottom floor, guest sleeping quarters and chill room in the middle, and master penthouse suite with revolving bed and retractable moon roof on top, plus a rooftop deck that could entertain up to two dozen hangers-on. Once it had been helicoptered into Hell's Bay, there were concerns that it might become mired in the marsh due to its excessive weight, so a few hours were spent bolstering the rig with flotation tubes for needed buoyancy.

After a dinner of lobster tails, chopped salad and boiled new potatoes, followed by chocolate mousse, black cherry pinot noir sorbet parfaits and copious flutes of Veuve Cliquot, Leland and Carmen retired to the master suite for one of those presumptuously intimate assignations that somehow escaped mention during the twelve episode seasonal arcs of *Sell Yourself.* Afterwards, Leland rolled his sweaty spread of billionaire flesh off her and settled into snoring sleep.

Carmen lay awake, wondering why she hadn't used Leland's fairly recent fourth marriage as an excuse to beg off, or at least insist that he put on a goddamn condom. She stared up through the moon roof into the sky, trying to focus on the wealth of constellations she hadn't seen since her Arizona girlhood. Her mind drifted to the protestors and crazy Scooter, and she wondered how much more money she'd need to accumulate before she was granted access to the switch that could shut down her own guilt. After all, it wouldn't do to have Leland suspecting that she actually empathized with those people.

She was startled from her reverie by a sound from outside. It took her a moment to recognize that it was Burke, barking tersely at someone out there in the dark. The next sound was louder, the distinctive firecracker *pop-pop-pop* of gunshots, flatter and less impactful in real life than in the movies. The third sound was an animalistic screech—possibly Burke. Carmen realized that she preferred to think it was Burke screaming than an injured or mortally wounded environmentalist kid. Stupid conscience.

A thumping at the door downstairs had her rolling out of bed and scrambling for whatever clothing she could locate. Surely Leland hadn't locked poor Burke out.

"Mr. deMand!" she whispered. "Boss! There's something going on!"

Leland grumbled something unintelligible and pulled the sheet up around his neck. The unspooled strands of his combover trailed out from one side of his head like the tail of an undomesticated beast. Carmen shuddered at the sight, turned and sprinted down the spiral staircase, almost losing her footing on the way.

The pounding continued as she made her way to the front entrance, where she stopped to peer through the peephole. Burke was there, expressionless and inscrutable as ever, though a little more disheveled than she was used to.

She yanked open the door and it struck her that while he was facing her, he also seemed to have his back to her. *Why do you have your suit on backwards?* she considered asking, but there wasn't time. He was already tumbling forward, his head twisted all the way around on his neck.

ר

Carmen's screams were what finally woke Leland from his near-comatose slumber. He lurched out of bed as disoriented as a bear post-hibernation, stumbling around the suite in search of his boxers.

The screams stopped abruptly, followed by a brief moment of unsettling silence. Then less recognizable noises, a wild animal's growl and a crashing, the sound of something desperate. Or hungry. Leland hoped the heavy footfalls coming up the stairs belonged to Burke, because anything else big enough to make that sound would likely damage the spiral staircase.

He smelled it first, a tear-inducing stench like wet dog, angry skunk, and the sulfurous reek of rotting eggs.

Then he saw it.

Seven feet tall at least, a dark silhouette of heavy-breathing rage, huge shaggy head scraping the low ceiling of the suite, impossibly long arms dragging on the floor. Leland started to laugh.

"You filthy hippy piece of shit!" he snarled. "Oh, man, are you ever going down hard for this. You think you're gonna scare me with a goddamn monkey costume? That is hilarious! I guess ol' Scooter really put some big ideas in your head. But you know what I'm gonna put in there? A fuckin' *bullet!*"

There was a gun here somewhere, but like his underpants, he would never find it, because the thing was on him, its hot foul breath right in his face as it let out a saliva-spewing roar that caused piss to dribble freely down his legs.

"Okay! I take it back! It's a very convincing costume. We could make some great videos, sell 'em to the tourists," Leland said. "Y'know...work together. Whattayasay?"

The creature grew quiet, cocking its head as it regarded him. Leland took that as an opportunity to bolt, leaping onto the king-sized bed and attempting to smash his way through the skylight.

The creature reached up and grabbed a handful of Leland's spilled combover, yanking him off his feet and dragging him off like a conquered cavewoman.

Leland bumped his way down the spiral staircase, screaming and struggling, but the thing's strength was tremendous, irresistible. As the creature pulled him toward whatever fate he had in store, Leland saw Carmen, still standing half-naked in the doorway, trembling and whimpering.

"Car...Carmen...*help me...*" he muttered through the blood on his lips. He'd broken a couple of teeth coming down the stairs, and maybe some ribs and an arm as well.

The creature paused in front of the terrified woman raised a finger to its lips, and made a gentle, slightly bemused *shushing* sound.

Carmen simply nodded in response.

Then the monster kicked Burke's twisted body out of its way, and hauled screaming Leland off into the endless murk of Hell's Bay.

FRIENDS WITH THE MOON

Amber Sparks

"There are still many who believe that the so-called Mothman that was encountered by dozens of residents during the 1960s was a bad omen, a shadowy portent of destruction, and that its manifestation spelled doom for all who were unfortunate enough to cross its path."

- Ken Gerard, *Encounters With Flying Humanoids*

It is earliest in the morning, that dark hour just before the sun. He is feeling his days as he makes wide circles over his own statue, a ridiculous metal thing that bears no resemblance to him at any stage of life. It looks like a cartoon superhero, muscular and upright and goggle-eyed. It has buttocks. Buttocks! If he knew how to laugh, he would. If he was that human, he might.

If his mate was still alive, she might remember how. She grew up in a copse of trees behind the high school; she was always telling him stories about the humans. They amaze him, these creatures. Their lives are so long but they do so little with them. As far as he can tell, they mostly drift, aimlessly, from building to building, and once inside, they sit and stare at a small flat box with bright pictures inside. Sometimes they press buttons to make the pictures change; sometimes they take in nourishment though bottles or cans while they watch.

The nectar makes them sleepy, mostly; but it also sometimes makes them wild and loud and unpredictable. He has to be careful around the humans when they get like this. It's when they're most likely to see him and do stupid things. His great-granddaddy thirteen times removed got himself shot trailing a pair of young humans. He wanted to observe their mating rituals, but instead he got a shotgun blast right between the antennae.

And he always, always travels at night. None of his people let themselves be seen by day anymore, not since the Incident. One of his mate's distant ancestors caused a terrible disaster when he perched on a bridge, curious about the strange armor the people don to travel long distances. No one was sure how it had happened, but the bridge chose that moment to collapse, spilling armor and metal and humans and all into the river and smashing a good many of them to bits. Some of the humans who lived saw the creature perched on the bridge before it broke apart. He was blamed, reviled, humanized, demonized—and his people could never be sure of their safety again.

Even now he is taking a terrible risk, flying out in the open like this, in the middle of the town square. But he knows he is dying; his wings hurt and his vision is going and he can't hear as well as he used to. This is his last flight, his solemn tribute to his only friend, the luminous pale moon. He knows that tomorrow he'll be dust, scales scattered over the sweet, dark earth—the only vital thing in this dried-up town.

The new moth's mother lays over 200 eggs on the leaves of the trees, each no bigger than a pencil mark. Inside, he and his hundreds of brothers and sisters wriggle and grow and finally eat their way free. He crawls to the edge of a juicy leaf, scrabbling and holding on with his many feet. Close by, the first humans he will ever see spread blankets over the grass, uncork a bottle of moonshine, giggle as the liquid hits the paper cups and the strong smell fills their nostrils. The caterpillar munches, unseen and unconcerned.

He has finally reached the limits of his appetite. He has split his own skin and has grown a new one, all the while filling his face with leaves, leaves, leaves. The sweet green taste is the only thing he knows, apart from the loud occasional steps and shouts of the huge creatures his elders call humans. He does not fear the humans as they do. He has grown and grown and grown, and is now the size of a large log.

He hides in the shadows of the oldest trees, deep in the woods while his brothers and sisters bring him many leaves as tribute. He understands that he has now become something apart – something not of the humans and not of the insects, something halfway in between. He will make a cocoon, and he will grow and change and emerge a new kind of creature entirely. His days as an ordinary moth are behind him, his consciousness expanding, widening as he begins to understand the world is larger than the wet logs and the shady trees.

He will need a mate, then, but that can wait. He will spend his days in sleep, his nights in flight, his once weak, wet wings a long proud span of aerodynamics and engineering. He will travel far, watching over the humans, too large to hear his own brothers and sisters' voices. He will make friends with the moon.

But for now, he is still eating, is still of his tribe, is still one creature among many. For now he can still swap stories of his kin. For now, he cannot imagine the dark empty sky, or the statue in the square, or any home besides the soil and the leaves and the silence of the oldest trees in the deepest forest.

WINGS, BONES

Lizz Huerta

*"Due to their supernatural nature, there are a few ways to guard oneself
against* La Lechuza. *A rope or string with seven knots serves as a talisman
against the creature. The services of a* curandera – *a Mexican shaman who
practices ancient Mayan healing techniques – may help. Prayer is also said
to work. If all else fails, shotguns seem to be effective against the creatures
– though after blasting a bird out of the sky only to have it transform into
the body of a woman, you'll probably have some serious explaining to do."*

- Scott Francis, *Monster Spotter's Guide to North America*

Mama, the only daughter in a tribe of sons, had left Texas at seventeen and only called
home on church holidays. She'd bow her head, listen to her old lady telling her all the
ways she'd gone wrong, all the curses coming up in her blood. The old lady I'd never
met would ask to talk to me and I would bow my head against the phone, while she
told me how good girls didn't leave home, not until they were wives. The old lady told
me I had to pray to the lady of the desert and Jesus for forgiveness. After those calls,
Mama and I would walk down to our Queen, let her waves crash on our feet, wash
away away the old lady's voice.

Hail, O Star of the Ocean was embroidered on the blanket Mama had made me when
was pregnant for me and dreamed I was a girl. Our Queen was the sea, her endless
names, and we lived down the street from Her. I'd sit on the shore, wrapped in my
blanket while Mama prayed in the waves. I couldn't surf as long as her, especially in
winter. Mama could ride every day, even after storms when the sewers from Tijuana
clouded the water. Our Queen was full of shit, literally, the day Mama caught death in
a cut on the bottom of her foot. We thought it was the flu, all aches and fever until she
stood up on her bed four days later and screamed. I rode in the ambulance. A social
worker showed up, she was so gentle with me I knew I was being prepared for the end
of my world. When they let me in Mama was not Mama, she was pale and there were
tubes and unfamiliar smells covering her.

An older trucker cousin in law I'd never known existed came for me after Mama was gone. We didn't talk much on the endless miles leading to Texas He had wanted to get home so I couldn't give Mama back to our Queen. I held her ashes on my lap all the days of road. When we got to Texas the old lady was what I imagined, puckered, clawed, imagining herself holy. She and I had looked at each other for a long while, I was looking for Mama in her face, she was looking for Mama in mine. *You must look like your daddy* she said finally and I shrugged and said *I look like myself.* Her lips went even thinner and she said *Oh you're her daughter all right.* I wanted to wash myself clean but there was no ocean near. I was as far away from our Queen as I'd ever been, and even farther away from Mama.

I was given Mama's old room, more a closet really. But there was nothing of her in it, twenty years gone. I put her ashes under the cot, back against the wall so no one would see her. There was a window, the sill outside covered in thick white bird shit. I saw the cousins for the first time out that window. The girl cousins, all legs and tossed hair, stepping dainty in a clique across the yard. The boy cousins squatted, spit and smoked and watched the girls.

The old lady yelled from her back door, the cousins came. The old lady hollered my name *Maya!* I went. The girl cousins tried to coo their way around me, clucking this and that about how sorry they were, how Mama was with Jesus. I saw greed in their hands as they went for my hair in the guise of pity, but really, they had taming on their hearts. The boy cousins smiled slow smiles at me and each other. They sniffed the air, squinted behind them at the sky and said *Storm coming.*

The old man died of a heart attack the night your Mama left, the girl cousins confided in me, and the old lady never forgave Mama. He'd left the house to Mama, who hadn't wanted it or anything to do with Texas. Why are there so many cousins? I asked a girl cousin. She said *We are Catholic. You named after those Mexican Indians, the ones who built the pyramids, said the world was ending?* I was surprised she knew even that much. *We're Mexican too,* I said. Her nose wrinkled and she said, *We are Texan and we love Jesus.* I told her I was named after the goddess of illusion, from the actual Indians in India. Her mouth went sideways and she told me to set the table. I saw her whispering later, all their eyes glancing back at me.

The storm came that night, like the boy cousins said. I watched the shit on the sill outside my room get washed away. I put Mama's ashes on the bed next to my pillow, between me and the wall. I tried not to cringe at the thunder and chattering rain. I didn't know storms. When it rained at home it was a safe rain, except for last time, when the rain carried death into our Queen and to mama. When I finally slept I dreamt I was looking for Mama everywhere. I went to our Queen thinking maybe Mama was riding. I drove from California to Texas and back with the windows open. She wasn't anywhere. In the morning Mama's ashes were wedged between the wall and the bed, the storm gone. *I will take you home,* I whispered to her. The window sill was again covered in shit. I looked closely and saw the shit was full of small bones.

I went outside, past the yard to where the prairie began. There the air almost smelled like our Queen, but less salty. The wind was almost like her waves on the grasses and I let myself ache for the first time since my arrival. Cigarette smoke came then, on the wind, followed by a drawled *Morning, Illusion.* One of the boy cousins, all winks and mockery. I turned away from him, back to the grasses but my Queen was gone. I hated Texas.

What kind of bird shits bones? I asked at breakfast. The hiss and chorus of *shhhhh* from the cousins startled me, someone kicked my leg under the long picnic table. They turned their heads, eyes wide, and relaxed when they saw the old lady wasn't near. The girl cousins tried to distract me into a conversation about California but I let my answers dull away any curiosity and they left me alone.

After breakfast I went up into the barn with the boy cousins who lured me with the promise of a good story. They told me about the owl, La Lechusa, they called her. *She's a witch*, they said. *She's cursed our family since before Texas had a name. She is a killer,* they said, *she is hungry for revenge.* I asked revenge for what. They laughed and said *Name it, she's a woman. She destroys.* They told me the night the old man had died, he'd been out looking for Mama. La Lechusa, they said, screamed at the old man, diving at him again and again until his heart exploded. The old lady blamed Mama for his death.

Later that day the old lady had a boy cousin take us into town in a yellow truck, just the two of us and him. We followed her from store to store where she bought nothing. She introduced me, *Tina's girl Maya*, and she collected pity and curiosity everywhere we went. *Bless her heart*, they all said and my heart got heavier with each blessing. She took us to a pink church at the edge of town, a garden of roses surrounded it. There a young priest gulped, sweat and said yes to her request, masses for Athena. *Tina*, the old lady corrected him, *Tina*. They negotiated while the boy cousin smoked outside. I wandered, remembering what Mama had told me about the three years between Texas and me.

Mama had wandered, with her backpack and wit. She said those years she learned to pray in the way of whatever land she had landed on. In Morocco she had covered her hair, in India she bent her body open, in France she let herself forgive her relationship with Mass. It was in Cuba that she'd met our Queen, following her, her waves south to Brazil. *But she is everywhere*, Mama had said many times, her hands moving though my hair, *you just have to look*. I looked then, in that pink church, but I couldn't find her. Maybe our Queen hated Texas too.

You're too much like your Mama, the old lady said on the drive home, her claws in the bare skin above my knee. *You need taming. I want you to spend time with your girl cousins and Jesus.* I said nothing. The girl cousins had Jesus and gossip, the boy cousins had trucks and mystery. I knew a truck could get me out of Texas, Jesus would only only hold me in place.

The uncles came that night and the old lady turned into another woman, and the girl cousins followed. They put on Texas music and ferried beer and food back and forth. The uncles hugged me too hard, tried to get me to sit in their laps and laughed when I refused. *Your Mama would have* they drawled and I had a feeling of why she'd left. One asked me if I knew anything about my daddy and another uncle said *A snake for sure.* I snuck a beer and went to the barn to hide, climbing up into the loft.

It was only kissing, but even a kiss is all the evil in the world when it isn't wanted and your arms and legs are being held down. The boy cousin who had driven us to town tried to use his whole body to kiss my whole body, his mouth trying to kiss my lips as his knees tried to kiss my knees, his hips my hips. Two more boy cousins held me and laughed. I screamed on the inside as my shirt was pulled up. I prayed for my Queen, begging her to come, or Mama, or both of them. *You're stupid Illusion, no one will believe you,* one said, his hands on my ankles. *Like your stupid Mama,* the one holding my arms over my head said. I got a leg free and kicked out, my foot hit something and it flew off the edge of the loft. The cousins let go of me, covering their heads with their arms as a shape half my size flew over us, wings kicking up dust with a cry that sounded like a woman's.

Lechusa! a cousin cried out as he scrambled down the ladder. The cousin on top me grunted, pulling himself off my body, *All you witches are sluts.*

I stayed there in the hay for a long while. My heart, heavy with Texas, was beating my blood so hard through my veins I was dizzy. I finally pulled myself up, wiped the saliva off my face, neck and stomach. I tried to control my shaking legs on the ladder. I went around the dark side of the house, through the side door, to my room. I pulled Mama out, curled myself around her until the shaking slowed and forced myself to sleep.

In my dreams Mama was calling me, I turned and turned and finally knelt. I heard her voice coming up from the ground and began digging. I came to a dome that covered the whole world. Looking into it I saw everything, I saw our Queen, how prayers floated up, creating Her. I saw Mama dancing with a snake around her hips. She was joyous, she looked at me and said *We are everywhere Maya, and in you. Look for us.* There was a crack, a burning on my spine. I arched backwards and screamed myself awake.

The old lady stood back from my bed with the broom she had used to smack me in one hand. My room was barely outlined in the morning light. I stared at the old lady. In one hand she held the broom, in the other she held Mama's ashes. I lunged for them but the old lady was quick and she held out the broom so that the handle hit me right in the chest. *Beer makes boys stupid and loud and I heard what you let those boys do.* The old lady's eyes shone with hatred in the half light. *Look at you, sleeping with your dead mama like some savage.* I pushed the broom away and tried to reach for Mama again, the cardboard box I had carried with me every day since she'd gone. The comfort of knowing her bones were close, even in powder, even in ash, was what had been holding me together since leaving California. *Mama,* I cried out and the old lady stabbed at me again with the broom handle. *Clean yourself up, we're taking your Mama to church this morning to pray some of her sins can be washed clean.* The old lady left, slamming the door.

I cried, finally. I hadn't cried in the hospital or in the foster home where they put me to wait for the relative to come for me. I hadn't cried on the drive from California or when the cousins held me down. But I cried then, the pain of where the old lady first hit me spread out across my shoulder blades, became hotter, went down my arms and I cried in pain. I cried for Mama, who had left me alone. I cried because I couldn't find our Queen. I cried because of the cousins, the way the uncles looked at me. I heard another cry, a soft call and I quieted. It came again, from outside. I opened the window and looked up into the eaves.

The owl was in the eaves, tucked into a nook. She was gray and white with feathers that looked like horns. Her yellow eyes stared into mine. She cried again softly, opened her wings and closed them. The sky was getting lighter, I saw her more clearly. The burning in my arms and back softened to warmth. She opened and closed her wings again, her eyes focused on mine. I opened my arms, awkwardly imitating her. She hopped from one foot to the other and cried out again, as if in approval. My heart, for the first time since Mama left, felt clear. I put my hands over my chest and whispered to her *Are you my Queen?* She blinked. Inside me something unfurled. The owl flew away.

Even the ride to town with the cousin who'd lay on top of me in the barn couldn't disturb my calm. I sat in the truck between him and the old lady, silent. The old lady sat stiffly, Mama's ashes between her and the car door, as if she was trying to keep Mama as far away from me as possible. I didn't care. I watched the road, the Texas sky with new, tears-washed eyes. I knew Mama wasn't in that box just like our Queen wasn't only in the sea.

The priest was awkward with Mama's ashes, holding them out from his body as he took them to the altar. The boy cousin announced he was going to take a ride over to the next county, to pick up some beer for later. He winked at me as he said it and a prickle rose on me, across my back, down to my hands. I kept my eyes on him until his sneer collapsed. He tripped on his way out of the church.

We're gonna pray now. Your Mama ever teach you how? The old lady grabbed my arm but I shook her off. I went to a pew in the back of the church The young priest began his ritual, the smoke. I glanced up to my left and saw I was sitting next to a statue of the lady of desert. I nodded at her, she was a Queen, even if she wasn't mine. I closed my eyes and began my own prayer.

I must have fallen asleep. I'd been dreaming I was soaring over the prairie, the grasses moved like the sea. The wind caught me and held me as I rode it like Mama had ridden waves. Below me were roads, dirt and asphalt shining in the heat. I saw a yellow truck I knew. I knew exactly who drove that it. I swooped low, flying impossibly fast until I was level with the driver's window. I reached out my hand to smack the window but I had no hands. Instead a wing reached out, tip feathers grazing the glass. His face went white, this boy cousin who had tried to kiss me with his whole body. He swerved his truck away from me. I flew up, up faster than he drove and turned in the air and rushed back, straight toward his windshield. This time when he swerved, he swerved hard.

The old lady smacked me awake. The priest was gone, mama was gone. *Shame on you, falling asleep at your own Mama's mass.* The old lady smacked me again, *Get up girl, your cousin should be on his way.* She walked away, muttering. I swallowed, coughed a little. My throat was dry and itchy, something was in my mouth. I wiped my index finger across my tongue and looked down. There was a feather there, small, gray, wet. I heard a siren, then another. I knew we would have to find another way home.

Beast Tours

Thomas Martin

"Hitting the papers in the slow news week after Christmas, the vampire Beast of Bladenboro gained an unusually large amount of attention. Hunters from as far away as Tennessee descended on the small town to see if they could get a shot at the beast. Newspapers from Arizona to New York ran coverage of the hunt for the creature. The town was engulfed in chaos, with men with guns walking through the forest shooting at anything that moved."

- Melissa Bunker, *Hooo... Yeah Boy!*

Until everything happened, I would have said Robby Howl was about like anyone else around here. He was a deer hunter and a bear hunter. He had a good set of dogs and he worked the mill straight out of high school.

But then the mill closed and he was married with a couple DUIs and an attitude that prevented him from working the few jobs that were hiring.

The mill had paid well and as a result Robby got spoiled early, developing a firm belief that his free time was worth more than what a shift at McDonalds or Hardees or Bojangles would pay.

So he lived off his severance package and then it was the unemployment checks keeping him going while he slowly completed court-ordered community service requirements at the Elizabethtown Animal Shelter.

Other than that he'd be out in the woods. Always out in those woods, running the dogs and checking the new trail cameras he bought with what was obviously his wife's money.

She was keeping them afloat, picking up extra shifts at the nursing home every chance she could and drinking a hell of a lot of Mountain Dew.

She stayed on him about getting a job, though. But it was pretty clear he was more than content with the way things were going.

This went on for a while.

But then the Monster Quest episode came out. And even though it profiled animal attacks all across the state, it was all based on the legend here in Bladenboro and Robby thought there might be an opportunity in what he expected to be a wave a publicity for the town.

And he wasn't the only one. The Boost the 'Boro revitalization committee was already planning a street festival dedicated to the fearsome bloodsucking creature that terrorized this area back in the 1950s.

So as soon as he could, Robby went to Staples for a pack of vinyl decals and right there in the parking lot, arranged the words BEAST TOURS on each side of his pick up truck with a cell phone number listed underneath.

And just like that, he was in business, ready to run trips in the spirit of those historic ghost walks you find in places like Charleston. But unlike Charleston, Bladenboro is not a coastal destination or, for that matter, a destination at all. It doesn't even happen to be on the way to a destination and that was a problem for Robby.

He had banked on the History Channel re-inspiring interest and transforming this town into something like the Roswell of North Carolina. But the show aired and time went by and it seemed no one was really moved to make the pilgrimage.

Worse than that, it was almost impossible to convince locals who knew the land and knew the legend to pay for a guided drive through the swamp with Robby pointing at patches of woods and reciting information from the Beast of Bladenboro Wikipedia page.

There needed to be something to make it interesting. Something to grab attention and fuel people's curiosity. And that's why I thought he reported seeing what he said he saw.

Robby called the North Carolina Wildlife Commission and went on about how it was nighttime and about how he was driving home across the county when he saw something just sitting there on its haunches, staring up at the sky. That's what he said, too. Said it was something just staring up at the sky. The thing was in the middle of the road, right on the yellow lines, and at first he figured it was bear just because of the size but the shape seemed too sleek for that so he kept inching closer in the truck till it broke its gaze and it turned its head and that's when he realized what it was. A mountain lion. Said that's the only thing it could've been. And then he said instead of that big cat getting spooked and jumping off into the woods, it just started running on down the road. So he followed it. And he saw the tail and the cauliflower ears and the shoulder blades moving in that alternating rhythm. He said he followed it for like 30 seconds with the high beams on before it realized it was not going to out run that truck. As soon as it did, though, with one swift motion, it turned to the right and jumped up about an 8-foot embankment, no problem.

The Wildlife Officer listened to Robby say what he said but as soon as he heard the call was coming from Bladen County, he laughed Robby right off the phone and didn't even bother going into how there hadn't been a confirmed mountain lion sighting in North Carolina for over 100 years.

And I bet that's what Robby expected to happen. I guess he just needed to lay groundwork. And after it was done, Robby went all over town preaching about how the Beast was back, how the Wildlife Commission didn't give a damn, and most importantly, about how he was ready to guide anyone through cougar habitat who was willing to pay.

He promised proof. And booked a few trips. And sure enough, claw marks and paw prints started showing up on the land he took tours.

Now I don't know how he got the cast for those cougar prints to look so realistic but I figure he just used a pocketknife to carve the claw marks in the trees.

He had his trail cameras set up on that land too and he checked them with each group midway through each tour. And every so often, they captured these blurry images of what had to be oversized house cats, preloaded on those cameras the night before.

Robby even had speakers stashed in the bushes that played recordings of these animal noises that sounded something like a woman being stabbed in the back. They were hid so well that nobody ever even stumbled over one of them but we all knew they had to be out there.

It was a great effort. It really was. And he played it brilliantly because not every trip would encounter tracks or hear noises. It was actually more often than not a tour would remain pretty uneventful. But that's what made it work. Robby operated like a parent on Christmas, taking bites from the cookies left for Santa, giving just enough to maintain an illusion people could convince themselves to believe.

He kept booking tours. Families and birthday parties and a lot of school field trips. Our state magazine even did a little profile on Robby, praising his ability create a tourist attraction in, what they called, a town emblematic of the region's slow decline.

Success came quick. And people started coming in from Raleigh and Fayetteville and Wilmington. But unfortunately that success wasn't sustained and the novelty of the whole thing just started to wear off.

That's why, at first, everybody thought Robby did what he did as an answer to the drop in attendance. But to this day, he claims he wasn't responsible and like everything else, puts the blame on that mountain lion he reported to the Wildlife Commission.

It was a 3rd grader from Bladen Lakes Primary School that found the first one. The skull was crushed. The jaw, detached. And most of the blood was drained from the body just the way it had happened back in the 1950s.

It was a stray dog no one claimed. And even though there wasn't any real evidence against him, it was too much of a coincidence that Robby had access to animals through his community service work over in Elizabethtown.

The rumor started almost immediately that instead of cremating dogs put down at the shelter, Robby had been stealing the bodies and staging Beast kills for his tours. And even though he completed those hours years ago, people seemed to have already made up their minds. Some said he still had a key from when he worked there. Others said he planned it all in advance and stored dogs in his freezer.

There were a handful, though, that believed him and agreed there had to be something fierce out there in the woods. A few big game hunters even contacted Robby wanting a chance to hunt the Beast. They offered him good money to guide them through the swamp but Robby turned every one of them down. He had closed the Beast Tours. And not because people weren't willing to go. His little stunt had worked. The interest was back and it only increased when more dogs around the county showed up killed the same way.

But Robby kept saying it was too dangerous to run tours and refused to take out any-one who asked. He never left the house, either, without a rifle on his shoulder and told everyone he saw to stay inside after dark.

For a moment there, people were nervous and thought there might be some truth in all his warnings. But then Robby's own beloved hunting dogs were found dead in his backyard and while he probably thought no one would consider him capable of such a thing, all those rumors made it easy to assume he was responsible.

Once word got out, news stations across the state were all over the story. PETA even got involved, demanding prosecution and sending protestors to picket outside Robby's house.

No charges ever came up about the dogs, though, and it seemed like Robby was trying to let it all blow over. He kept to himself for the most part during that time and cut out all that talk about some sort of Beast running wild through the county.

Time went by. And when no more dogs were found, the protestors eventually started packing up and it was almost like things were about to get back to normal around here but of course, that's not what happened.

They found his wife out in the woods on a Sunday morning with Dan Beason of Dan Beason Toyota. She was naked and Dan had his pants around his ankles. Both their bodies were gutted. Skulls crushed. Jaws detached. And paw prints were all around the scene.

Now, from what I understand, Robby acted appropriately conflicted when receiving the news that his wife was not only dead but had been running around on him while getting that way. They said he seemed about as upset as a man should be, given the situation.

But the police got a warrant anyway. And when they searched the house, they found some pictures on Robby's computer he probably should have deleted. Pictures from those trail cameras dated prior to when Robby started the Beast Tours. Pictures of his wife and Dan Beason looking like teenagers in the bed of a Tacoma parked on a deer trail somewhere out in the woods.

They arrested him. And Robby's serving time now. He's still claiming the Beast is out there. Still saying he had nothing to do with any of it. But ever since he's been locked up, no tracks have been found. No attacks have been reported. And no noises have been heard in the night. Nothing else has happened. And I think even he knows, deep down, nothing else will.

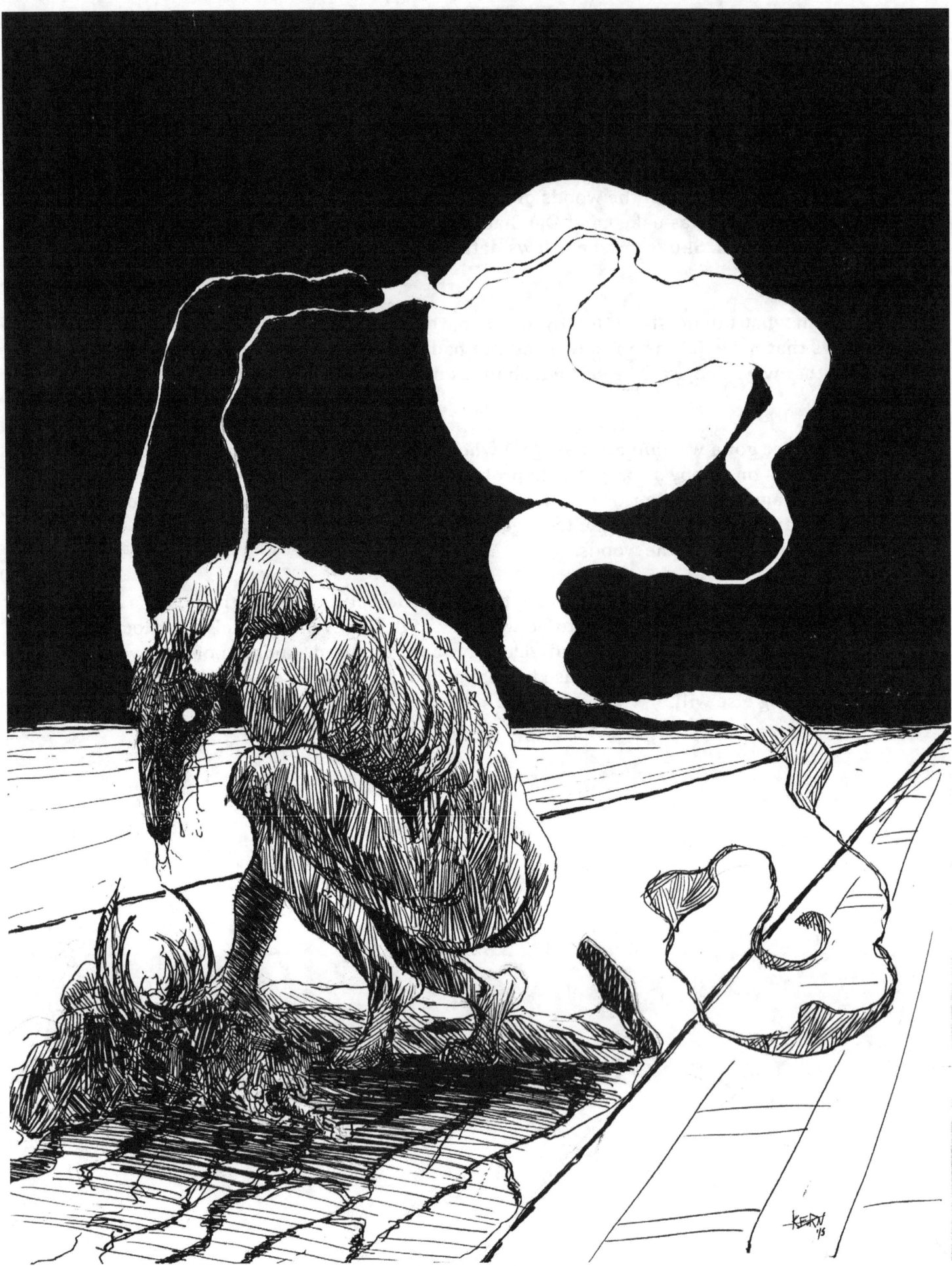

Different Monsters

Steve Jones

"There is one well-known, never-explained 1971 sightings flap involving a "wolf woman" in Mobile, Alabama. The Mobile Register received over fifty calls in April of that year claiming that a creature that looked like a woman on its top half and wolf on its lower parts roamed Davis Avenue by night. People say it was hairy but oddly pretty, and it chased a man from a marsh. I'm not sure this is the same creature as the upright canines, however, since dogmen are not usually described by witnesses as having human faces or torsos."

- Linda S. Godfrey, *Real Wolfmen*

Deputy Sheriff Dawes flicked the switch for the bubble flasher on the top of his patrol car as he pulled onto the shoulder behind the old Ford. This stretch of Route 22 was little more than a country road, and barely traveled at this time of night. Dawes was thorough, however, and included this area in his overnight patrols. It seemed that tonight the extra attention had been worth it.

He stepped out of his car and thought, *How in hell did this truck make it all the way from Arizona?* He guessed it was a '58 or '59 Ford. The original color was lost between various expanding rust tumors. The cab's back window had a thick crack from one corner to the other. Both rear tires were nearly bald and the fronts were even worse.

The truck's door creaked open and his hand tightened, just a bit, on the handle of his .38. Then a woman climbed out.

"Wow. I'm glad to see you," she said.

Deputy Dawes relaxed his grip, but left his hand resting on the butt of his revolver. "Car trouble, ma'am?" he asked. He saw her eyes flick down, just for a moment, to his gun before she answered.

"Yes, sir," she said. "I'm afraid it could be my generator. I can't get it to turn over at all. I don't suppose there's anyone out tonight with a tow-truck?"

The top part of Dawes's mind was able to keep this conversation going with only the slightest delay in his responses. The other part, the *deep* part, was still lagging behind, stuck in the moment where she had climbed out of the truck. She was attractive—even in the harsh light of the patrol car's headlights he could see that—but that wasn't it. Something else danced around his head just beyond his grasp. He had a troubling feeling that there was something he was missing.

"Officer?" she asked, and the question echoed through his thoughts like a stone tossed into a well. Two more seconds stretched by until finally he managed to respond.

"It's Deputy, ma'am, Deputy Wade Dawes. I'm sorry if I'm a bit distracted. We've had us some unfortunate occurrences of late here in the greater Mobile area. Coming upon you stranded out here like this, well, I'd be glad to make sure you get somewhere safe."

"Thank you, Deputy," she said and smiled at him, but was there something in her dark eyes. All at once he felt like this was a situation where he was two or three steps behind.

"I was asking if there was anyone we could get to tow the truck into the city?" she said.

"I'm afraid not, ma'am. We just had a wreck out on I65 and both of the fellas I'd normally look to call on this late were out there. Just where were you headed, if you don't mind my asking?"

"My sister lives in Prichard," she said. "That's where I was going. I think I got turned around trying to read my map in the dark."

Now it was his turn to smile. "I'm driving down to the office in Mobile. Prichard's on the way. I'd be happy to give you a ride. I'll have the truck towed down in the morning."

She said her name was Alexis King. Before she got into the car with him, she collected her purse and one bag from the truck and thanked him again for his offer.

They settled into the car and he began driving. She explained that she was in Alabama to visit her sister who'd left Arizona two years ago "to follow a boy." The way she said those four words told the whole story. Since then, "the boy" lost his job at the paper mill and had lit out, leaving her sister with a stack of bills. Her sister had stuck around Alabama, working to pay off their debt, and she was registered at the University for the fall semester.

Alexis spoke with obvious love and pride. She finished her story and paused for a moment before saying, "So, Deputy. You mentioned 'unfortunate occurrences' back there.

I take it you mean the murders?"

At first he was surprised, but then he realized he shouldn't be. The story had become national news. Over the last four months the bodies of five young women had been found around the Mobile area. Everyone in his department was pulling long hours and working with the city police department, and state police, but so far there were no leads.

"My sister told me about it," Alexis continued. "It was just another reason for all of us to try and talk her into moving back home, but she wouldn't hear it. She always had a rebellious streak. It drove my folks crazy."

Dawes settled into his seat and listened to her talk. At first thinking about the murders had stirred him up, but her voice was soothing, and stealing glances at her legs was nice.

"Now, on top of the missing women you have reports of a werewolf."

Dawes could hear the teasing playfulness in her voice, and felt himself flushing. The damn "Wolf-Woman of Mobile" was the latest headline he'd seen. Once again he knew he shouldn't be surprised. Once the reporters had come into town following the murders, keeping the local stories about a "Wolf-Woman" a secret had been impossible. Last he heard there had been over thirty reports in the past two or three days. All of them reported around Davis Avenue in Plateau.

"That's just nonsense, ma'am. To be honest, we aren't focusing much attention to the idea of a half-woman, half-wolf running around."

"Come on, Deputy," she said, as she turned to look at him. "You don't *believe* such a creature could be real?"

He glanced at her and chuckled before returning his eyes to the road. He had to admit, if only to himself, the Wolf-Woman made a much better conversation than the missing women. "No ma'am. I don't believe in vampires, Frankenstein, or the Wolfman--or Wolf-Woman, in this case."

"Still," she said. He thought he heard the humor fall away from her voice, replaced by a coldness. "It is odd, all those reports coming in, all very similar, and all in that area."

Dawes didn't look away from the road this time, but he had that feeling again of being two moves behind. It reminded him of when he used to play chess with his grandfather during summers on the lake. His grandfather had insisted he'd learn the game, and Dawes had taken to it. Still, he never got to his grandfather's level. Even at the end the old man was still sharp, still thinking several moves ahead of Wade.

"Is that right, ma'am?" he said. "I haven't had time to listen to the news lately. Just what is it they're reporting?"

"They say she's beautiful," Alexis said. "Isn't that a strange way to describe such a thing, 'beautiful'?" That's what they're saying though. Most people have run away from her, but those that approach always lose sight of her, and then she's gone."

"I imagine that's because it was never there in the first place," Dawes said.

"Maybe it's a ghost," she said. This time Dawes was sure there was no humor in her voice. It unnerved him. This conversation had lost any sense of pleasantness, and he didn't like her tone. Her words seemed to hang there with implications. He felt like her comments were directed to him.

An uncomfortable silence stretched between them. He realized he was starting to sweat just a little, and turned up the car's fan.

"You must have been following the wolf-woman story pretty closely," he said, probing.

"Have *you* ever been to Davis Avenue?" she asked. "It's not all far from Prichard, is it?"

It took a degree of control to continue driving without reacting, but Dawes was practiced in control. At least, he was *most* of the time.

"I just realized," he said, struggling to keep his conversational tone. "You never mentioned your sister's name."

"It's Becca," Alexis said. "Rebecca King."

Dawes's face was a mask, seemingly concentrating on the dark road, but his mind was racing. He was thinking of the cabin, his grandfather's old place on the lake, where they'd had so many chess games. It was his now and he tried to make it up most weekends in the summer. Under the floorboards in the back bedroom he kept a metal box with a few keepsakes. He had one from each of them.

The papers knew about five dead girls and the police suspected three others might be connected, but the real number was much more than that. His first one had been when he was just fifteen. There had been times when he had convinced himself he was done with it. Then he would start again, and wonder how he had ever thought he could quit. He spent many hours going through his keepsakes, replaying each experience. With the keepsakes in his hands he found he could remember every detail.

He thought about the last thing he'd put in the box. It was a scarf with the initials RK on it. She'd been walking home, still wearing her waitress uniform. She'd been pretty. He always picked pretty girls, but it had been the scarf that really pleased him. For the first time since he'd seen her face, he felt in control. Her face had troubled him so because it was familiar. It wasn't the same, of course, but the similarities, once seen, could not be denied. There was a grim satisfaction as the puzzle piece he'd turned over and over in his mind finally snapped into place.

He stomped the brakes now and pulled over to the shoulder, throwing the gear shift into park before the car had even stopped. He'd never pulled his sidearm from this position. For a moment he thought he wouldn't be able to get it loose from the holster, but it came easily. He cocked and leveled the gun at her in one motion and held it on her.

She moved before he could react. Her left hand was a blur, and before he could register that anything had happened his right hand sang briefly with pain, before going numb. His gun tumbled to the backseat. He turned to go for it when she began to speak.

"I can still smell her on you." She pulled in a long breath through her nose. "I can smell *all* of them."

There was something in that voice that made him turn back to her, even as parts of him cried out not to. He looked and felt his world begin to slip away. The woman who had got into the car with him was *changing*, like some nightmare come to life. A sound, both guttural and somehow pleasurable, came from somewhere within her. A snout began to emerge. Teeth that had no place in a human mouth actually grew into place. He heard a wet, snapping sound as parts inside her broke and shifted into a new, inhuman shape. He saw her pores open as coarse black fur leapt outward, and smelled the animal musk that poured from her. He felt the moist heat of her breath as she moved toward him.

Dawes felt heavy in his seat. His gun was a forgotten artifact and lost forever just out of reach. Somewhere in the middle of it all, before her legs had completely reformed in their new crooked shape, she spoke to him. Her mouth, working with some difficulty due to its new structure and oversized teeth, began to form slow, terrible words.

"I will send you to Hell with your guts dragging behind you."

Then she was on him. He got his right hand up in front of his face, and his left pressed against her torso. He felt that thick mat of hair covering her body and shuddered. His hand brushed against something and he realized with sudden nausea that it was her nipple.

Her snout pushed forward toward his throat. He tried to get his right hand up to perhaps grab it but her jaws snapped, and his fingers disappeared into her throat. Blood poured from the stumps as he pulled the hand away, trying to comprehend this sudden reduction of himself.

Her hands had him pinned now against the driver's side door. He felt claws dig into the flesh of his shoulders. The pain was enormous, but it was quickly replaced as agony burned along his midsection. He saw some movement and realized her back leg was working. She was tearing him open along his belly. He tried to scream but couldn't seem to get any air into his lungs. All the while she kept flexing and extending that leg, sending those claws deeper into him. Blood was splashing onto the dashboard now. His belt let go and this time she sent the claws deep into him. She tensed and flexed. As she moved through him he realized he was being damaged in a way that could never be repaired. At one point he felt her claws click against bone before she was through. His entire midsection had been replaced with a flaring, wet hole.

The car filled with the smell of blood and shit. His hand left her body and, seemingly of its own volition, reached to probe the damage.

Grayness was beginning to creep in around the edges of his vision. His hand had left his ruined abdomen and seemed to float in front of his face. Perhaps it was some last effort to ward her off. He watched with some detachment as his hand disappeared into her dripping, biting muzzle. He heard sounds, as though through a long tunnel, and a felt a flash of pain in his arm that pushed back the grayness a bit. He blinked and his hand was gone.

The rest was a series of sensations between longer and longer periods of darkness. There was pain, like lightning streaking across a night sky, but it seemed to be getting further and further away. Once he felt her teeth around his face and the undeniable truth of what she was doing to him threatened to bring him back, but he realized with grateful relief it was much easier to just let go and stop caring.

She's eating me up, he realized, but by then there was no horror, just a tired acceptance. Then, even that was gone.

A

Deputy Dawes's car was found the next day. An autopsy determined the cause of death to be wolf attack, despite some rather glaring questions about how such an animal could have gotten into his patrol car. His cabin was not searched. The box beneath the floorboards was never found.

THE WEST

OREGON ◼ CRATER LAKE
NIGHT TOUR

WASHINGTON ◼ THE BATSQUATCH
BATSQUATCH

NEVADA ◣ TAHOE TESSIE
ONE DAY IN JULY

SAN DIEGO, CA ◣ THE PROCTOR VALLEY MONSTER
FIELD MANUAL

IDAHO ◣ THE MASSIVE WOLVES OF IDAHO
ESTO PERPETUA

NIGHT TOUR

Zack Wentz

"They warned people about the monster living in the chilly depths of Crater Lake, but no one believed them."

- Andrea Lankford, *Haunted Hikes*

From: **Canoe Captain** (canoecaptain@dreamcanoeadventures.com)
Sent: Mon 06/13/14 6:47 PM
To: Central Management (centralmanagement@dreamcanoeadventures.com)

Dear Center Manager--

Wizard Island is unreal! Wish my dad could be here. Seriously. Crater Lake's the most beeeeeeeeeeeeeeeeautiful place! \(^0^)/

Like I said in my resume/e-mail thing I've seen TONS of water. Lakes, rivers, creeks, oceans. Name it. And I thought there'd be people everywhere, almost being summer, but there's no one. Beautiful.

Gabe gave me the co. phone and said Canoe Captain's supposed to report to Central Management, but didn't tell me who I'm supposed to address so apologies in advance for the un-personalized salutation :-\

Got picked up fine. Larson did the driving (didn't say his first name, unless that IS his first name LOL) and Gabe told me all the Crater Lake trivia for wowing tourists (Giant! Crawdad! Dragons! 8-O). Larson's quiet. Maybe surprised by me being younger than them, weirded out I'm their new "boss." (&_&)

Anyway, Wizard Island really does look wizardy, and from the cabin you can see a corner of Phantom Ship. Tomorrow I'll try to find The Old Man of the Lake, and practice the balancing routine (to wow tourists ;-D).

Canoes aren't in the greatest shape, but I *think* I can fix. Watched my dad do ours a ton. Gabe said someone broke into the cabin over the winter and stole some things, but there's a few decent canvas scraps here. Worse case, use a ton of duct tape :-P

My dad and me sometimes went out on stuff that barely floated and slept in just jackets, so this is practically a luxury resort. He worked the lookout tower on Indian Ridge for the Forest Service, and sometimes wouldn't see another person for weeks. Said it was the best time of his life. I thought he was crazy, but I think now I get what he was talking about. How the Indians or whatever thought it was "sacred." Wow.

Anyway, thanks for this totally amazing summer job. Not to "overshare," but things weren't going super great back in Grants Pass, so when you answered my e-mail to your ad for Canoe Captain so quick it was a GODSEND :-)))

Jamie K.

Canoe Captain--DreamCanoeAdventuresInc--Crater Lake

∎

From: **Canoe Captain** (canoecaptain@dreamcanoeadventures.com)
Sent: Mon 06/13/14 7:02 PM
To: Central Management (centralmanagement@dreamcanoeadventures.com)

Center Manager—

Please accept my apologies for the previous e-mail. I understand Canoe Captain is a position that entails serious responsibilities. From now on I'll strive to maintain more professional behavior.

I guess everyone I've ever talked to online said I was TMI (Too Much Info), but I guess that's probably TMI right there to even say so. Sorry.

I'll immediately look into why numbers have been down in recent seasons, fix the canoes, and get back with a full report.

Again, super sorry. :-(
Jamie K.

Canoe Captain--DreamCanoeAdventuresInc--Crater Lake

◼

From: **Canoe Captain** (canoecaptain@dreamcanoeadventures.com)
Sent: Tues 06/14/14 3:41 PM
To: Central Management (centralmanagement@dreamcanoeadventures.com)

Answers to the initiatory quiz you just sent. Report to follow.

1. Crater Lake wasn't made by a meteor. It's a caldera lake, from a volcano called Mount Mazama that erupted almost 8,000 (?) years ago. Caldera's from the same Latin root as the word cauldron (sorry, forgot exact word).

2. Both the Modoc and the Klamath had myths about a battle between Skell, sky god, and Llao, god of the underworld. Mount Mazama was where their realms connected, and after they fought and Llao got killed Skell tricked all of Llao's lake dragons to eat his body, but when they saw the head they realized they were eating their master and left it, so Llao's head became Wizard Island.

3. Besides salmon and trout, local animals include Roosevelt Elk, Mule Deer, Black Bear, Mountain Chickadee, Bald Eagles, and sometimes Golden Eagles. There's also, of course, Sasquatch, and Llao's lake dragons, which are supposed to look like block-long black crayfish, and at night reach out of the water and grab whatever foolish braves (or tourists) try to camp on their master's head (ie Wizard Island). Pretty cray-cray crayfish LOL. ((:.:))

4. Old Man of the Lake's what's left of a Hemlock Tree, about 30 feet tall, that's been floating around at least a hundred years. It's been recorded drifting as much as 60 (? pretty sure) miles over three months.

5. Phantom Ship's a natural rock formation named because that's what it looked like to the first explorers. It's about 500 feet long, almost 200 feet tall at the peak, has lichen and wildflowers, a few different kinds of trees, and some swallow colonies.

7. Sorry, but totally dunno the answer to this one. Gabe didn't say anything about it. Sounds insane and super messed up, but I'll ask him, and promise to memorize the answers to all the other stuff. Didn't know there was gonna be a quiz.

As far as my report, Gabe thinks things fell off last year because there's another canoe tour "poaching" our customers. He thinks they broke into our cabin and trashed the canoes and stole stuff, and he'd tell me more later.

Sorry, but that's all I know. If I could get online I could do some research, but for some reason this phone only works for e-mailing your address. Doesn't work for making calls, searching the internet, texting, writing anyone else :\

Fixing canoes is going okay. I found some duct tape.

Jamie K.

Canoe Captain--DreamCanoeAdventuresInc--Crater Lake

★

From: **Canoe Captain** (canoecaptain@dreamcanoeadventures.com)
Sent: Tues 06/14/14 10:07 PM
To: Central Management (centralmanagement@dreamcanoeadventures.com)

Again, sorry. Totally understand your annoyance, and didn't mean to seem to be foisting blame onto crew, if that's what I was doing. I understand we're a team, and take full responsibility. Super sorry.

And yes, I understand Dreamcanoeadventuresinc's policy for employees to carry no personal electronic communication devices. I was just suggesting I could help more re: why numbers were down.

That said, I think I might've gained some insight into the whole thing. Larson went to get more supplies this afternoon, and said he'd be gone overnight because he's gonna "drum up some business" for us. First time he's talked to me.

After Larson left Gabe came down. He thinks there's a secret "night tour" canoe co. that started last year. Basically what we do, but night, and goes out to Wizard Island. I asked him why he waited to tell me, and he said, "We'll just see how much business Larson drums up while he's in town." Then it was nothing but Native American legends, UFOs, Bigfoot, disappearances around the lake going back to Gold Rush days. (=_=)zzzz

Gabe just went to bed, so I'm staying up watching Wizard Island to see if I can spot anyone out on the water.

Jamie K.

Canoe Captain--DreamCanoeAdventuresInc--Crater Lake

★

From: **Canoe Captain** (canoecaptain@dreamcanoeadventures.com)
Sent: Tues 06/14/14 11:47 PM
To: Central Management (centralmanagement@dreamcanoeadventures.com)

Okay. Definitely saw something. There's lights on the island. Water's just dark, but there's someone on there for sure.

Jamie K.

Canoe Captain--DreamCanoeAdventuresInc--Crater Lake

■

From: **Canoe Captain** (canoecaptain@dreamcanoeadventures.com)
Sent: Weds 06/15/14 6:47 PM
To: Central Management (centralmanagement@dreamcanoeadventures.com)

I regret to inform you that I'm offering my resignation, effective immediately. I'm guessing something like this must've happened with your last Canoe Captain.

Larson pulled up at about 7:30am. Gabe had just got up and was a ways down the bank. Larson got out as I was walking to the truck and went right past me, straight toward Gabe.

I followed Larson, saying I needed to talk to him, but he just kept walking. I was starting to get frustrated, so I just asked straight up if he's part of a night tour, taking away our business. I *might* have suggested he'd broken into the cabin and trashed our canoes.

Larson spun around and threw me in the mud. Called me black robe, custer, maggot, moon cricket, monkey, white eye, wasicun, wailing on me, and I didn't know what to fucking do. I kept putting my hands up and he'd knock them away, then he dragged me to the lake and stuck my face in the water. I thought I was gonna die. Felt like a full minute until he let go.

Gabe and him were fighting and it was like I wasn't even there anymore. I started puking water, seeing fuzzy black stuff out the corners of my eyes. It didn't seem real.

Look, I'm not gonna try to sue you guys or anything. I just need a ride or ticket back to Grants Pass. Sorry to have wasted your time. I just wanna go home.

And, honestly, I don't think either of these canoes is gonna float. They're both too far gone.

And, for the record, I'm NOT some paleface honky. My father was ONE EIGHTH Cherokee. Tell that to fucking Cray-Cray Horse.

Last, I haven't appreciated the way you've written to me since I've gotten here. Whoever answered the ad was way nicer, and I don't think you understand what it's like in my position. I feel like you've been super mean and rude, and if someone would've written to me in that tone from the beginning, I never would've taken the job.

Jamie K.

Canoe Captain--DreamCanoeAdventuresInc--Crater Lake

◼

From: **Canoe Captain** (canoecaptain@dreamcanoeadventures.com)
Sent: Thurs 06/16/14 2:13 PM
To: Central Management (centralmanagement@dreamcanoeadventures.com)

Dear Stacie,

Wow. Thanks SOOOOOOO MUCH for your awesome e-mail! I had NO IDEA you were my age. Sounds like we have a TON in common. Can't believe we even work for the same place. It's crazy. (O_O)

Totally understand why you had to be all serious and anonymous. It's your job. And thanks for the compliments on my old profile pics #-) I never go on there anymore, and actually was super out of shape in most of those (going through weird family shit, eating a ton). Anyway, sounds like you know all about how things are on the crazy-fam front. Super sorry. And hey, I'd love to see a pic of you sometime ;^D

Anyway, felt better after reading everything you wrote and went and talked to Larson and he seemed like he felt bad. He got a bunch of whiskey in town (Old Crow! (XOX)) and I caught a pretty fat trout, so tonight we're gonna bury the hatchet or whatever. Maybe we'll carve a to-tem pole. [(8){:{O}:}X]

I'll write you back tomorrow, and again thanks TONS for your e-mail, Stacie. Seriously. You rule :-D

Jamie K.
P.S. super sorry about how things are going for you back home (swear it'll get better!).

Canoe Captain--DreamCanoeAdventuresInc--Crater Lake

◼

From: **Canoe Captain** (canoecaptain@dreamcanoeadventures.com)
Sent: Fri 06/17/14 9:27 PM
To: Central Management (centralmanagement@dreamcanoeadventures.com)

Hey Stacie--

Tried to write you last night after everyone passed out, but was seriously too messed up. Soooooooo hungover {{(+_+)}} We polished off all the Old Crow, and did some serious smoking of the peace pipe :-?

Larson's actually super cool. Just intense. He said he's Klamath and how warriors in his tribe swam the lake and climbed Llao's head on Wizard Island for power. But then Gabe went and put his foot in it, saying how his ancestors knew the island wasn't meant for men, and even looking at the lake could steal your soul.

They totally went at it. I guess Gabe is almost full Modoc. Anyway, I broke it up, and they calmed down and Larson said he had something to show us so we went in the woods a ways.

There was this huge White Pine, and behind it Larson pulled back this big brown tarp and there was this crazy painted monster face. Front end of this gigantic dugout canoe. Maybe 20 feet.

Larson said he'd built it himself. After his old lady kicked him out he came up, and when he saw the cabin had been broken into and the canoes were damaged, he just started "channeling the energy of his people."

Looks like the kind of thing it'd take two guys a year to build. Gabe wanted to take it out right then, but we were all way too fucked up (* ,*) so I decided to be captain again and said we'd do it tomorrow after we got some sleep (-.-)zzzzz

Sort of expected backtalk, but they were both totally cool with it, so I guess tonight we're gonna check out the island and see what's going on with this supposed "Night Tour" and all those lights.

Love,
Jammers
P.S. Think you could maybe send a pic of you? :^D

Jamie K.

Canoe Captain--DreamCanoeAdventuresInc--Crater Lake

From: **Canoe Captain** (canoecaptain@dreamcanoeadventures.com)
Sent: Fri 06/17/14 10:38 PM
To: Central Management (centralmanagement@dreamcanoeadventures.com)

Holy crap, Stacie, you should be a frikkin model or something (6_6) Serious. TOTALLY want to meet in person after the season's over. After seeing your pic, wishing it was already over now 8-)'

I'll get the phone good and charged in the truck for when we go to the island, and update you real-time with everything. If Larson or Gabe get offended, I'll say it's a direct order from Center MGMT ;-}

Okay. Better get ready!

xoxoxoxoxoxo
love,
Jammerz

PS *3*

Jamie K.

Canoe Captain--DreamCanoeAdventuresInc--Crater Lake

◼

From: **Canoe Captain** (canoecaptain@dreamcanoeadventures.com)
Sent: Sat 06/18/14 12:16 AM
To: Central Management (centralmanagement@dreamcanoeadventures.com)

Man, weird to not be paddling. About a third of the way across to Wizard Island or more. Larson's paddling up front, Gabe behind, and I feel kind of shitty to not be paddling, but they didn't even ask.

Anyway, seeing lights again, but it's strange because it's not like they look any bigger or closer. Hard to tell what they are. Not like fires, or lamps or anything. Just this glowing.

No clouds. Crazy how loud the quiet is. God, the water is so clear. Even in the dark with just stars and moon you can see at least twenty, thirty feet down. Totally amazing. Wish you could be here :}

Funny, now that I think of it, but of all the times me and my dad went out on the water we never went at night.

Jamie K.

Canoe Captain--DreamCanoeAdventuresInc--Crater Lake

From: **Canoe Captain** (canoecaptain@dreamcanoeadventures.com)
Sent: Sat 06/18/14 12:28 AM
To: Central Management (centralmanagement@dreamcanoeadventures.com)

Holy shit a huge black thing size of a building just went under us. Canoe's still rocking like crazy. Larson and Gabe won't talk. Just keep paddling. Must've taken a full minute to pass under. Jesus what the hell was that?

Larson and Gabe won't fucking talk. What the fuck? Stacie this is fucked.

Stacie, I'd really, really like to hear back from you. Anything, if you're there, okay? :-(

Jamie K.

Canoe Captain--DreamCanoeAdventuresInc--Crater Lake

From: **Canoe Captain** (canoecaptain@dreamcanoeadventures.com)
Sent: Sat 06/18/14 1:12 AM
To: Central Management (centralmanagement@dreamcanoeadventures.com)

Okay. On the island. No lights or anything. Just quiet.

Gabe and Larson still won't talk. Maybe freaked about the thing that went under as I am. Seriously, it was this huge long black shape, wide as a house, maybe 15 feet? Just kept going and when it was gone there was all kinds of wake happening. Just fucking crazy. Sturgeon don't even get that big. Nothing gets that big. Maybe whales? Is there a black whale? Black freshwater whale?

We're gonna split up and go around the island. Meeting back here at the canoe. Larson thinks the other co. camp out here, and that's what those lights are, but there aren't any lights now I can see.

Please write something back, okay? Just anything.

Jamie K.

Canoe Captain--DreamCanoeAdventuresInc--Crater Lake

◼

From: **Canoe Captain** (canoecaptain@dreamcanoeadventures.com)
Sent: Sat 06/18/14 1:41 AM
To: Central Management (centralmanagement@dreamcanoeadventures.com)

Almost at the top. Haven't seen anything that looks like it was a campsite. Honestly, doesn't feel like people come here at all.

Can't see shit on the water. Even from this high still looks pretty clear.

When I get up top I'll do a 360. Seriously, should be able to see that thing. Shadow of it, or something. It was moving toward the island.

Stacie, I'd really like to hear back. Feeling really freaked and alone. I don't feel like we're supposed to be here. Feels like nobody's supposed to be here.

Jamie K.

Canoe Captain--DreamCanoeAdventuresInc--Crater Lake

◼

From: **Canoe Captain** (canoecaptain@dreamcanoeadventures.com)
Sent: Sat 06/18/14 2:03 AM
To: Central Management (centralmanagement@dreamcanoeadventures.com)

Can see across to where I think our cabin is, but can't see it. There's Phantom Ship. Can't see Old Man. Really doesn't seem to be anyone here. Can't see Gabe or Larson anywhere either.

Stacie, I don't think I want this job anymore. I mean, is our company really even legit? Is it cool for someone to be doing private canoe tours here? Haven't seen anyone on the lake at all. Rangers, tourists, anything. Just the lights on the island that aren't even here now that I'm on the fucking island.

Seems like if it was really okay to be doing canoe tours, there'd be people all over the place. There's seriously no one.

Stacie, please, what the fuck is going on?

Jamie K.

Canoe Captain--DreamCanoeAdventuresInc--Crater Lake

◼

From: **Canoe Captain** (canoecaptain@dreamcanoeadventures.com)
Sent: Sat 06/18/14 2:57 AM
To: Central Management (centralmanagement@dreamcanoeadventures.com)

Shit my throat is tore up from running all the way back down and shouting. Stacie, Gabe and Larson are gone. Canoe is gone. There's NOBODY on this fucking island but me and it's freezing. I know it's supposed to be summer, but can't even feel my feet anymore. Stacie PLEASE fucking help. Why aren't you answering?

Jamie K.

Canoe Captain--DreamCanoeAdventuresInc--Crater Lake

◼

From: Canoe Captain (canoecaptain@dreamcanoeadventures.com)
Sent: Sat 06/18/14 3:39 AM
To: Central Management (centralmanagement@dreamcanoeadventures.com)

Stacie phone's gonna die. When you read this when you wake up or whatever, I'm on the island. Please send someone. Swear to God I can see that shape moving around in the water again, but can't say for sure because I'm too freaked. It feels like the sun's never gonna come up.

Stacie, please, please, please, please.

Jamie K.

Canoe Captain--DreamCanoeAdventuresInc--Crater Lake

◼

From: **Canoe Captain** (canoecaptain@dreamcanoeadventures.com)
Sent: Mon 06/18/15 2:39 PM
To: Central Management (centralmanagement@dreamcanoeadventures.com)

Attn: Center Manager,

This is Tennille Powers, new Canoe Captain hire for your Crater Lake crew.

I've arrived at the campsite, and was given this phone and instructed to make contact with you by the guide with the longer hair (name starts with G or J).

At any rate, so far so good. I've only recently moved out to the West Coast, so this is a very different sort of outdoors environment for me, but I like the feel of it. This place has a lot of atmosphere.

The long-haired guide seems to lay it on a little thick with all the legends and spook stories, but I assume we need to have a handle on all that to entertain the tourists. I suppose the majesty of the great outdoors sans sensationalism isn't enough to wow all of them. Sign of the times.

That said, I think I'm really going to enjoy the work out here.

Thank you again for the opportunity.

Best,
Tennille P.

Canoe Captain--DreamCanoeAdventuresInc--Crater Lake

BATSQUATCH

Kirsten Alene

"Some people theorize that when Mount St. Helens erupted, it also opened a dimensional portal, in which the Batsquatch entered. Descriptions of the Batsquatch are that it has the head of a bat, red eyes, purple skin and the wings of a pterodactyl."

- Paul Dale Roberts, *H.P.I. Chronicles, Volume 1*

When my grandmother finds him I am too young to know that he is not like other cats.
My experience with animals is limited.
I am six.
A picture of a porcupine recently blew my mind.

His name is Pussy.
We're about the same size.
We play together a lot during the first few months. I like the look of his human-y face.
He has deep-set, reddish eyes and a heavy, neanderthalic brow.
He likes my Tonka trucks.
We make some mud pies and he eats one.
His front paws are big and awkward ("because he's only a kitten," explains my grandmother) and a tissue-thin skin flap extends from his clawed paws to his haunches ("all cats have that when they're born," she says).
He hoots as well as meows. But his meows are pretty aggressive.

Now I am sixteen and I know Pussy was not like other cats.
My grandmother is dead and my mother asks me to drive to the cabin and collect some things. She's busy with work and plus, the place gives her the willies.

"And do something about Pussy," she says as she's cramming a sandwich bag in through the partially open passenger side window.
"How do you know Pussy is still alive? That cat was weird as fuck," I say, rolling the window down a little more. The sandwich bag plops onto the seat.
"Your grandmother mentioned him in the will."

We stopped visiting shortly after my first few encounters with Pussy. My grandmother started coming over to our place, which my mother said was safer. The cabin was a disaster and Grandma had all these game snares and bear traps set up in the yard. It wasn't an ideal environment for a six year old.
I think the final straw was when I walked into a tangle of fishing line hanging off the wall and a barbed hook stuck in my eye.
My mother was pretty mad. Grandma seemed unsurprised.
Pussy licked the blood off my shirt.

The cabin is in worse shape than I remember, but then ten or so years have passed and there was only Grandma to keep things up. The closest neighbor is over fifteen miles away, on the other side of a sizable river that cuts through the outer reaches of the property.
It takes me ten minutes of driving back and forth along a one mile stretch of road to find the driveway.
"Your destination is on the left."
One second later.
"Turn around. Turn around. Re-routing."
Then.
"Your destination is on the right."
One second later.
"Turn around. Turn around. Re-routing."

It looks like part of the roof has caved in. There is a tarp over the front window, the porch is at a 45 degree angle. A tree appears to have grown through one wall.
I sit in the car in front of the house for a while, eating the contents of the sandwich bag: a stale slice of bread, two honey packets from KFC, and a coke.
She's a better mother than that would seem to indicate. It's the end of the month and money's tight.
In fact, I wish I was going in to retrieve some sort of jewelry box of valuables or a

cache of hidden dough, but grandma was about as poor as we are. All she had were her car (which is going to the cost of the funeral) and this cabin (pretty much worthless as you can imagine).

Anyway I think after about a quarter of an hour it's time to rip the bandaid and get this unpleasant task over with.

I keep reminding myself that she died at the casino - not here - and that there's no conceivable way I will encounter a body.

I slam the car door.

Couldn't possibly be any sort of body.

Which is hard because the cabin looks like a crypt or at least the setting of a very gritty, realistic horror flick.

As I attempt to safely navigate the dilapidated staircase, I hear a loud bang from inside the place. Something falling over.

Probably raccoons, I say immediately out loud, trying to head off my own imagination. The door's not locked and the screen is kind of drooping off the hinges.

Holy shit.

It smells.

It smells so bad inside this house.

It smells like a corpse rotting at the center of a two month old, sedan-sized plate of deviled eggs.

I resist the urge to run to the car and never look back. But then I think of my mom at work, nervously checking her phone under the counter, waiting for me to get back in cell range and tell her I got that old set of China and the photos of grandpa that she wants.

I think of the starry look on her face every time she talks about that goddamn China. "It survived the San Francisco earthquake...twice!" (Twinkle twinkle).

"It's alright. There is not a body in here," I say aloud, though I am now reasonably sure, based on the smell, that there are several. Raccoons or possums or maybe a lonely old bear that has crawled in here to die.

I dig around the kitchen and every sound I make gets echoed back to me from somewhere deeper in the house.

There's no electricity, so I'm using my cellphone as a flashlight and it's pale white light isn't doing the kitchen cupboards any favors. At least one raccoon has been here...for a while.

After opening every cupboard (no China), I move to the rooms at the back of the house, thinking it might be packed away under a bed somewhere.

Ugh.

Under a bed. Anything could be under these beds. I hope for somewhere more obvious. The creaking floorboards get louder and louder as I creep down the hall.

Then there's another sound.

Some sort of metallic clanging. This clanging is not related to my footsteps.

I don't have too many memories of this place, but I do remember the room I used to stay in. There was dinosaur wallpaper and a plastic bat hung from the ceiling like a mobile. The shadows of it swinging around used to wake me up terrified at night.

I reach for the doorknob.

Initially, I think I've surprised a squatter. What a squatter would be doing all the shit way out here is anyone's guess.

The door bangs open.

This guy is eight feet tall. His head is brushing the ceiling. Or where the ceiling would be, but it's caved in a little and light trickles down onto this mottled brown and black skin that hangs in ribbons off his hairy hairy body. Red, red eyes and a wormy white grimace.

The guy is as petrified as me and neither of us move.

Then he makes this terrible hooting sound and I start screaming and the worst thing happens: he raises his arms, like, to grab me I guess, and these ENORMOUS black and tan flaps fly out from his sides like two family sized beach umbrella. He flaps the umbrellas and hoots.

I am stunned into silence.

He lunges at me again, but I can see how he's chained to the bedpost, which looks like it's bolted to the wall. A huge, industrial padlock is clamped over the chains wrapped around the bedpost.

We both sort of stand there. He's not a squatter. He's some sort of huge gorilla man. And his skin isn't shredded. He's wearing some tattered pants. They're a bit too short on him, his legs are tremendously long.

Oh god.

He flaps his umbrellas again.

Holy mother of god.

He's now meowing like a cat.

"Pussy!?" I scream, much louder than I intend.

He stops flapping at once and the dust settles.

He looks terrible. Like he's been chained up here for ages. But for a while at least, someone was feeding him.

There's the China, laid up in neat stacks, all crusted with the remains of food. What looks like some moldy waffles and a piece of hairy meat.

"Whoa," I say.

"Whoa," says Pussy in imitation.

My first thought is to run. So I run.

I slam the door and tear down the hallway, slamming into the wooden stove and almost breaking both my ankles by launching myself down the crooked staircase.

I am in the car. I lock the doors.

I have been in the car for twenty minutes.

I think: "Should I call animal control? The humane society? Is there some sort of protocol for this?"

No, they would probably shoot him.

Hell. I would shoot him.

The government?

That would take forever. He'd probably starve. If he wasn't already starved too bad to recover. He looked like a rotting skeleton. Ew.

I'm not very clever and I don't have a lot of other ideas, so I go back inside.

It's not for the China.

Fuck the China.

We'll burn this place down and if the China survives, we'll pluck it from the wreckage. But that thing's chained up and it's going to die.

I can hear it moaning and mewling like a cat again.

Shit.

I wonder if it will kill me and eat me as soon as it's loose.

Back in the house, there's a key on a nail outside the bedroom door that looks like it could open a padlock.

So I grab it.

I run inside, diving through the filth. I slide to the bedpost, unlock the lock (miraculously on the first try), and scramble back out, my heart racing so fast I think I'll black out.

But I don't.

The hooting starts again. But I'm already back in the car.

I'm already back on the road.

I'm going the wrong way but I don't care.

"Turn around. Turn around. Re-routing," says the car.

"Shut up. Shut up."

That's when I see it, kind of hunched on the side of the road, once again looking like a crusty homeless dude with some baggy umbrellas under his arms.

It's Pussy.

He straightens up, unfurls his wings, and flaps into the sky. He's silhouetted like a huge bat, like the bat symbol. Like a big gorilla man with wings.

I swerve into the other lane, over correct, spin the car, and come to a temporary backwards stop.

Damn.

I don't even care.

I slam on the gas and squeal off down the road in the right direction, watching Pussy get smaller and smaller in the rearview.

He's dipping and diving in the oncoming dusk.

I wonder if he's catching gnats or something.

One Day in July

Cameron Pierce

"According to online sources, there have been numerous Tessie sightings over the last seventy years or so. But none have been substantiated, and Tessie's true identity, not to mention her very existence, remains entirely speculative. Still, I bet there isn't a swimmer who has dived into Tahoe's deep blue waters, especially in the middle of the lake, that hasn't peered past their toes into the deep blue and wondered...."

- Tracy Salcedo-Chourre, *Best Hikes near Reno and Lake Tahoe*

One day in July, my mother and I took the bus to Lake Tahoe in Nevada, where my uncle was getting married. My father didn't go with us because he was sleeping on the couch at the time on account of their not getting along. They could hardly make it through dinner without fighting, so a road trip was out of the question. Anyway, the family rented this big cabin on the lake and we all stayed there together, my grandmother and my aunts and my cousins and even distant relatives who I'd never met. The first night my mother and I arrived, the adults drank beer and us kids played and we were a family.

The next day, everybody went out to breakfast at a crepe house on the lake. I was pretty stoked about that because my father always made me crepes, but at this crepe house on Lake Tahoe, I learned that what my father called crepes and what the rest of the world called crepes were two different things entirely. My father's crepes were regular old Bisquick pancakes, filled with slices of butter and rolled up like a burrito, then buried in a mound of powdered sugar. What this restaurant did was something else. I guess you'd call it more authentic, but I liked my father's crepes better.

After we ate, some of us went into the gift shop next door, which was filled with souvenirs and T-shirts all featuring the local lake monster, Tahoe Tessie. My mom bought me a book about Tahoe Tessie and also this handheld game where you tried to shake these plastic balls into Tahoe Tessie's mouth. I read the book on the drive back to the cabin, then I read it again sitting on the porch, looking out over the lake and feeling equal parts wonder and dread as I considered the possibility of coming face to face with the Lake Tahoe monster. I read the book again that evening before bed, and that night, I dreamed of Tahoe Tessie. Her long, slender form shot out of an underwater cave, heading straight at me, and I opened my mouth to scream only for my mouth to fill up with water, and then I woke up.

My mom came into the room and found me crying. She tried to soothe me, but I could still see the smooth, dark skin of Tessie, her eyes kind but the ragged teeth in her mouth telling another story.

The next day when everybody went for a swim in the lake, I remained on the beach, digging my toes in the warm sand. I was too afraid. They called out to me to join them. My mom came out of the water and asked me if everything was fine. I told her the hot dogs we'd eaten for lunch made me sick. She believed me and returned to the water. I had to will myself not to shout for her, to beg her to stay out of the water. Tahoe Tessie was going to get her. I just knew it.

My mom wasn't eaten by Tahoe Tessie that day. Nobody was.

The wedding was in three days and all I could think now was, *How are we going to get out of here alive?* For all I knew, Tahoe Tessie could invade dreams. Maybe if I hadn't woken up, my mom would've found a bloody mess in the morning. Not wanting to dream of Tessie again, I tried not to fall asleep that night. The family had set up one room for all of us kids to sleep in, so there weren't any adults around to tell me to go to sleep, and all the kids drifted off soon as their heads touched their pillows, like babies. On one hand, I wished someone would stay up with me, share my fear of Tahoe Tessie. On the other hand, I liked being alone. It felt good. But sitting up all night with nothing to do got boring, so I started reading my book on Tahoe Tessie again. The illustrations depicted her as this smiling turquoise dinosaur thing, but I had seen the true Tessie in my dreams. She was serpent-like, gargantuan, her flesh slimy and dark like the weird catfish my brother had caught the week before while we were fishing for yellow perch at the gazebo on Lake Stevens.

Something howled outside and I threw myself under a blanket. I knew it had to be Tahoe Tessie howling out there, and that meant she could go on land, and that meant I was a goner.

The next thing I knew, I was waking up. I hadn't died and everything was still fine.

"Get up," my mom was saying. "We're going boating."

I protested. I feigned sickness. My mom was having none of it. "Your uncle is bringing fishing rods. You love fishing. Get dressed and meet us outside."

I started to cry when she left the room. Luckily all my cousins who were staying in the room had already gone downstairs. I guess I'd slept through the first wakeup call because I'd stayed up so late.

I put on my favorite T-shirt, the one with flying sharks on it. My dad dressed me in that shirt the one and only time my family ever went to church, which told me everything I needed to know about their feelings on religion, but crying alone in a room in a cabin, desperate not to get eaten by Tahoe Tessie, I thought maybe my parents knew something I didn't. Maybe they'd dressed me in my flying shark shirt in order to infuse it with some special religious protections or something, like as long as I wore this T-shirt with flying sharks on it, I wouldn't die. I stopped crying, realizing I was invincible. *Bring it on, Tessie*, I thought, probably squinting my eyes in this way I used to because I thought it made me look tough.

I guess somebody had gone down to the marina to rent some boats already, because when I went outside, everybody was piled into one of three different speedboats. I had to wade out to climb into the one with my mother and grandmother and Uncle Jeb, who wasn't really my uncle or anyone's uncle, but everybody called him Uncle Jeb because he was family and nobody knew what else to call him.

I didn't even mind wading out in the water because I knew my awesome T-shirt would protect me.

I climbed into the boat and we sped off, one boat after another, and it felt good.

Uncle Jeb used to live not too far off from Lake Tahoe in the town of Truckee. Whenever he had time off from building cabins in Truckee, he'd drive to Lake Tahoe to fish, so he knew the lake well and seemed excited to show the whole family his good spots.

Well, on the way out to the good fishing spot, Uncle Jeb was speeding a little too fast. We hit some rough chop and everybody's clinging on for dear life, but I was so little then. I couldn't even play tackle football yet because I was under the league's weight requirement. The day was early but Uncle Jeb was already drunk. That's the only thing that could explain what happened next. He lost control momentarily, sliding from his seat to the floor of the boat, which nearly capsized but righted itself at the last moment, only too late. I was pitched out into the cold, deep lake. I was a decent swimmer, but getting thrown out of the boat from a high speed, I skipped along the surface of the water like a stone. The impact stunned me, and so when I began to sink, I sank fast. Limbs flailing, I was going under. The surface fled from me like dreams of a happy family. I opened my mouth involuntarily, desperate for air, and my mouth filled with water.

Then without warning, a serpentine darkness sped toward me in the blue water.

As if out of my nightmare, Tahoe Tessie had come for me. Unlike my nightmares, Tessie did not eat me or spill my blood. Instead, she coiled her tail around me and swam away with me, toward a distant shore.

I awoke an unknown time later on a remote beach, sputtering, coughing water from my lungs. Hours passed before my family found me. Lake Tahoe was big and I'd wound up a very long way from where I was thrown overboard.

Everybody was impressed that I'd managed to swim all that way. They looked at my scrawny pale body with a newfound admiration.

FIELD MANUAL

JS Breukelaar

"'Proctor Valley Road is just one of those places where a vortex is bound to happen... That first night, a group of us next to the power plant saw a coiled rattlesnake on the side of the road, immediately afterward we saw this huge dark figure that looked like a Sasquatch coming straight toward us, some of us ran after it and then it just dissipated!'"

- Sally Richards (personal interview)

Jack Devlin and Dickey Alford were fourteen and thirteen respectively when their daddies came home from the war. Two years later Jack's old man was running for chairman on the incorporation ticket and Dickey's daddy, who served with the 2nd Combat Engineer Battalion out of Camp Elliot, had spoken no more than a dozen words to his son since *The Star* ran that stark front page: 'PEACE.' You've seen how it works in these small towns? How war puts a bony finger to the lips of the hard men who return, hammers something untouchable into them, something undiscoverable like no matter what they told you, it would never be all there was.

The boys grew up on dairy farms on opposite sides of the brand new reservoir between San Miguel Road and Otay Lake, right here in Bonita. On that late summer day in 1947 that Dickey would make the monster, both boys were on their horses. Whose idea it was to leave their bikes, that part of their boyhood, behind—and what it had to do with Jack having turned sixteen in May, or the extra glob of grease Dickey had taken to combing through his pale hair—neither yet could say. The sky was leaden and the ground muddy after the rains, tar weed thickets hissing with insects and frogs. Passing the reservoir, all pale and shiny like the back of a throat, Jack felt hot under his hat. From up ahead, Dickey's pale hair flashed silver between the branches, and his croaky braggadocio came floating back to Jack in snatches, talking about a girl called Kit.

Kit worked as an usher at the Odeon in Chula Vista, wore a soiled blue skirt and a matching hat. She smoked Chesterfields and drove a 37 Ford truck that belonged to an uncle back in Idaho she didn't like to talk about. Dickey was saying about whether or not it mattered that Kit was so much older than him—nineteen—and about that mysterious man she was dating in Jamul, the one that kept her in perfume and earrings and an occasional black eye. And then, moving between topics with his usual dexterity, Dickey wondered how many bridges he could have blown up in the war if only he'd been old enough to enlist.

"Main thing," he said, over his shoulder at Jack. "What I read it in my brother's field manual, is not to fail."

"Fail at what?" Jack said.

Dickey slowed a little, pulling a tattered book out from his back pocket. "'Failure of a single demolition could cost the lives of hundreds of men,'" he quoted cheerfully. "Give me half a box of C4 and I'll show Jerry what fails all right."

"Smokestack Joe to boot," said Jack, and they laughed.

Now this was at the cusp of the post-war housing boom, when most cow country folk wanted nothing to do with progress, figured no more was needed in the valley besides a controlled flow of illegals to work the farms that ringed the reservoir, and an elected official committed to keeping both the developers and the Jap citrus growers out in equal measure.

Jack saw how Dickey sat awkwardly on his saddle, due to the field manual he'd returned to his back pocket. Dickey was a reader. Leastways he wasn't no cowboy, he said—that was his brother's job, before he got blown up in Corregidor, and everyone knew they'd argued about it. How instead of doing his chores, Dickey'd sneak off to read about genetics and Sumerian cuneiform, or some new medical condition, or conservation, something no one spoke about back then. Dickey'd talk Jack's ear off about star systems and killer whales—how they'd mate for life, how the male dorsal fin would collapse in captivity, and how the females live almost twice as long and run the show. Jack didn't mind, anything was better than listening to Dickey talk about Kit.

But the point where their horses crested the rise that looked east across Proctor Valley, Dickey was back to saying how by the time you're in your twenties, it wouldn't matter who was older. A girl like Kit would take up all the air in the room, he said, even in the morgue.

"What about Mae?" said Jack.

Dickey shrugged. Mae was Kit's younger sister. She was in the same class as Dickey, and Jack had seen how she looked at his friend. But the truth of it was that on matinee Saturdays, there wasn't a male over the age of twelve in the dark of that theatre whose mind wasn't on Kit's soiled blue skirt and who couldn't smell her perfume over the greasy reek of popcorn, and taste her sugar in their sodas or dream about it.

Jack had almost caught up with Dickey over the rise, when he heard the sound. A moan, not quite human. Jack's mare froze, and Dickey's horse pulled up short.

The moan came again. Jack saw it then, a stricken heifer from behind a cluster of oaks on the hillside to their left. Dickey steered the Pinto through a gap in the wire fence, got there first, but already Jack knew what the trouble was.

"It's dead inside her," Dickey said.

Gooseflesh lifted on the back of Jack's neck right under the dark hair he got from his Mexican mother and which Kit liked to grab by the handful beside the reservoir where they met when they could. Cattle nosing around the truck, the coolness of her skin beneath that crinkled blue uniform. How her hips jutted into his belly, the way she didn't mind how hungrily he feasted on her and how there was always more. No end to what they had, so long as they were careful, so long as they didn't give it a name. They never talked much when they were together—let the meteor showers or rumble of the dam speak for them. But when they did talk it was mainly about how Kit had saved up almost enough to get to Hollywood, or the latest outbreak of cow fever, or whether Sheriff Almirez would catch that wildcat or whatever it was mutilating illegals. What wasn't said, what stayed unspoken between them was that Jack could date whoever he wanted and that Kit'd never stop seeing Dickey's old man once a week at the Desert Flower Inn over at Jamul.

She made Jack promise not to tell, said that it was for Dickey's own good—what he didn't know couldn't hurt him. Jack stared down at the road winding away below them, through what Dickey called no-man's land, where the green vegetation thinned to sage scrub, juniper and the occasional abandoned serape all the way to Jamul. Tried not hear the heifer's moans.

"We got to get it out," said Dickey in a voice gone deep and quiet.

Problem with watching a cow give birth is that the calf, when it has pushed its way through the birth canal and is emergent from the mother's body, problem is that it looks like nothing on earth. Jack had seen it hundreds of times, had himself roped and pulled the alien issue from that gushing hole, still he couldn't abide it. How until it struggled into being from where it lay all twisted and blood-cauled in the dirt, what came from the mother cow could have been anything. A monster, a rocket, a man.

"Foreleg is missing," Jack said.

All you could see sticking out from under the heifer's tail was the eyeless head. A triangular mass, slick with blood, all angles like something broken. The heifer was on her side and this time the sound that came from her was more like a scream.

Dickey jumped off his horse and went over to her. She tried to get to her feet, flopped back down in the dust. When he went at the thing beneath her tail, she clipped him on the hip with her hoof, put him on his ass.

What people don't realize is how big a Holstein is up close, especially compared to a stunted, pimply runt like Dickey. Dickey approached again, dwarfed by her haunches and that veiled obscenity refusing to budge from where it had lodged, half in and half out, neither one thing or another. Jack swore as Dickey plunged both arms in, pulled them out slick with goo, and stepped away from her hindlegs. Looked up at Jack frozen in the saddle.

"We'll have to rope her to the tree." Matter dripped from Dickey's twitching fingers.

Jack had grown too big for basketball, had half a head and twenty pounds on Dickey, but said he'd rather ride to the Schultz's—it was one of theirs—and call for a vet. Dickey said there wasn't time, she'd be dead by then. So Jack got off his horse, catching his foot in the stirrup on the way down. Stumbled on one leg before pulling himself free. Face burning, he picked up his hat from where it had fallen, grabbed a rope and went over to the cow.

"Not my idea of a fishing trip," he grumbled, but Dickey's attention was focused inward, an airtight set to his mouth like their daddies got when they were riffling through pages of the almanac, but really seeing faces sheared by shrapnel and limbs unclaimed in foreign mud. Both arms deep inside the heifer, he was rummaging for the foreleg, trying to reposition the calf so he could pull it out.

Jack knew it to be a bull.

He got the rope around the heifer's neck but not so it would choke her, and he tied her legs and then looped the rope around the oak. She ignored him, her black irises tumbling around a tiny core of blue at their center.

"Talk to her," Dickey said. "Tell her it's gonna be okay."

How many times had Jack heard his daddy say the same thing to his men during bad calvings? Had them on their knees, murmuring encouragement—blessings, prayers, or confessions—into the straining ear of the mother caught between the need to expel and the need to retain the creature she had made. Jack did not feel up to the task. Kit had not yet made a man of him, and Jack wondered if that was ever her intent—so instead he joined Dickey and loosened the hind legs somewhat so that the heifer could still bear down. Dickey's arms moved more surely inside her now, pulled out the calf's wasted foreleg. Jack watched Dickey hug both skinny arms around the calf's neck, Dickey's feet churning in the mud while Jack put a shoulder to her rump. Dickey and the calf were head to head and all but kissing—the calf's tongue lolled but its unformed eye was fixed on Jack. The mother's legs stiffened and the calf gushed forth in a mess of blood and afterbirth, gunk still spilling out of her as Dickey landed on the grass with the calf on top of him. Sat there for a moment dazed with the thing sprawled in his lap.

The heifer had gone silent, craning her head to see what the world had taken from her, and how she could follow it to wherever it went.

Jack walked around on wobbly legs to untie her. She lay still, except for a tremor that rippled along her coat like lightning along a rug. Dickey pushed the calf into the dirt and stood. They both looked down at it, the sharp corrugations of its ribs, three legs balletically sprawled. Its pelvis looked savagely flattened, maybe crushed in the birth canal, that blind eye criss-crossed in blood.

After a while Dicky smoothed greased hair off his forehead, and his lips hung loose and damp the way they got when he was discussing Halley's comet or Kit's laugh. But what Jack saw was that in the course of delivering that dead bull something had changed in his friend, so that for a moment it wasn't Dickey that stood beside him with that creature between them, but Dickey's dead older brother, the natural born cowboy, come back from the war.

"Are you thinking what I'm thinking?" Dickey's voice was as hollow as his eyes.

Trouble with a question like that between friends, is that it was what Dickey would call rhetorical. Jack was thinking the same as Dickey, that what felt worse than war was the shapeless, unending silence of peace, and whatever its prey, illegals from Mexico or cowboys on the shores of Corregidor, or a movie usher called Kit from Idaho, it made sense to give it form. To lay at its feet, like an offering, the blame for what, to a man, they'd become. So that's what they did.

At first it was just a few slashes with their hunting knives across the calf's body, but then the cuts became hacks and the hacks became amputations and rearrangements until what was left was as unrecognizable as, splattered hat to heel in blood and shattered bone, they had become to each other.

Laughing until they cried, pointing at each other's red war paint and spiralling in the mud, Jack forgot about the heifer, forgot about everything so that it was not until they dragged what they'd made over to the wire fence and strung it up there with entrail and vine, and felt the first drops of rain, that they saw that the mother had gone.

"Who cares?" Dickey said, wincing a little on his bruised hip. "She'll be back with the herd."

Jack wiped away his tears with a bloody sleeve. Agreed that what with the size of Schultz's ranch, and the man power still not sufficient to work it, even with the Mexicans, a pregnant heifer could have easily escaped notice.

The rain was a blessing, but not enough. Still hiccoughing in short humorless bursts, they churned up the mud to cover their prints, cleaned themselves off in a shallow watering hole at the edge of no-man's land. Jack dove in fully clothed and skimmed the silty bottom, pushing turtles aside with his blood-smeared hands.

"What if we get caught?" he asked Dickey, wringing pond water from his hair.

"Got to take the bull by the horns," Dickey giggled. He bent down to retrieve his brother's field manual from the mud, tucked it under the saddle.

He explained that they needed an alibi, and then they'd make up a story about a monster in the valley, and how they'd seen it themselves—strung up on Schultz's fence. Jack said, "What'll we call it?"

Dickey shrugged. "Proctor Valley Monster?"

Jack shivered in his wet clothes. "Sounds dumb," he said.

But it worked. Next morning they told some kids at the drug store and some toughs outside the gas station, smoking and sitting in their trucks. Dickey called Mae on the telephone and told her, and Jack told it again at football practice, about the thing they saw slung up on the Schultz's fence. Soon there were cars of sailors, trucks loaded with kids driving in to get a glimpse of the Proctor Valley Monster.

A few days later Jack's mother said at supper time how Lottie Schulz had found a dead heifer at the watering hole, no sign of disease or predator.

"These things happen," Jack's father said. "Animals die of natural causes, too."

"Nothing natural about a heifer just keeling over for no reason."

Newly elected District Chairman John Devlin Sr. winked at his son. "Women and cows will do as they please. Sooner we men get used to the idea, the better. Eh boy?"

A week later when Sheriff Almirez went to take the thing down off the fence, it had gone. No sign of it on the fence, not a hair. Dickey and Jack swore to the Sheriff, and to each other, that neither had anything to do with its disappearance, and as much as each wanted to call the other a liar—how else to explain the new distance between them—they both knew better. Hoof prints in the mud, the Sheriff took care to mention, calling on both Jack and Dickey's parents, were all that was left.

And then one night, it must have been early December—his mother's baking had already begun to fill the house—Jack and Kit were in her truck beside the reservoir, wrapped in a blanket. Kit was crying for some reason, silently, so that the sound of hooves came clearly to Jack from outside the truck. He listened for a while to the uneven thud that retreated and returned, whatever was out there making circles around him. Kit had drifted off, her eyelashes clumped with tears. Jack removed his arm from around her shoulder and rubbed a patch of steam off the window. There outside in the dark, with the mouth of the reservoir behind it, stood a young bull. Its forehead was pierced by one horn, the other pointing toward the moon like a jagged fingernail. Favoring a phantom foreleg, it stood canted in the vaporous light, lathered in moonlit sweat. Blood dripped from a cracked muzzle, and Jack could see its innards squirm from between a gash in its chest. One eye seeped. From the other glowed a blue light which fixed on him, until lowering its shaggy head with a dancer's grace, it turned away, hindquarters naked and hairless, its sex almost brushing the ground.

The Proctor Valley Monster made the town a little bigger, a little louder. People from outside came looking for it, reporters and thrill-seekers. They spoke, on both sides of the border, of how the Proctor Valley Monster had scared off whatever had been killing the Mexicans and some hailed it as a miracle. The silence lifted for a time, so it wasn't long before Dickey got wind of rumors, too. Rumors that led him to follow Kit in her truck to the reservoir, where he saw her with Jack.

What happened after that was never discussed. How Jack's best friend, Dickey Alford set three blocks of C4 explosive on the roof of the Devlin barn that Christmas Eve of 1947, detonated the charge with a pull lighter from sixty yards, and then turned his dead brother's defence weapon on himself.

The Colt failed to fire. A dud round, most likely, said Jack's old man, who refrained from laying charges, said the Alfords had lost enough already. But Jack knew then that the monster had found Dickey too, just not what form it had taken, and he never got the chance to ask. Jack and Dickey would both have the opportunity to serve their country in Korea, but only one of them would return. Mae's first job as District Chairwoman was to open the Lt. Richard Alford Jr Memorial Library right here in Bonita where the fire station is now.

Last time Jack saw Kit was that night in her truck, the night the monster found him. He may have read about her once or twice in the movie magazines but has since forgotten what they said. He still lives on the family farm, what's left of it, an old man now, older than old. Clint Eastwood old, he likes to say with a chuckle, burning across no-man's land in his big F-250, headlights turning the road red as a vein, ahead of him a dark silhouette and the lopsided thunder of hooves.

ESTO PERPETUA

Heather Fowler

"The Idaho wolves will be turned loose as soon as they arrive, to see if they will adapt as readily as some biologists believe to be possible. It is all an experiment, never tried before."

- Thomas McNamee, *The Killing of Wolf Number Ten*

I'm human. What does this mean? It's been five winters now that I've run with adopted wolves, traveling with a pack. I don't tire easily anymore. They lope and I lope. I wear the same North Face hiking boots, the same green Cabela jacket and threadbare Levis. My long brunette hair tangles in the wind. My boots hit the snow like jackrabbits darting, and, in winter, my breath makes clouds in the white-grey sky.

Like this, my memory is opaque for whatever came before, thaws here and there and then refreezes, like ice from fair days locks up frosty after nightfall. All I know now is these wolves, though their pack is always in flux. There is no spoken language; I don't diminish them by assigning human names. There are seven of them.

When they howl, I howl along. When they bark, yap, growl, and moan, I join. They permit me to linger near and mark their territory. There is beauty in the simplicity of our communal ways.

The life of wolves is lived in the moment. Wolves communicate with tone, expression, the movement of tails, decisive action. When I am with them, I, too, live in the moment. The alpha bitch is my favorite. She lets me sleep beside her, nestle in her fur. I hear the blood move in her heart. She's a strong alpha. My bond's with her as if our pulses were joined.

I left most of my humanity behind before I ventured to join them, enjoyed my solitude hiking over hills—as I still do. I still carry my pack and provisions as I shadow them. On days I hear humans in the woods, sometimes, I remember my old job, my old ways.

Once I was an ecosystem researcher. I used to care about having money and making a family. I used to have a lab and a name and a pregnancy and a man. The name means nothing on this terrain. The pregnancy self-terminated. The man's name was Timothy, but he's dead to me now, too. He's probably on some campus and found himself a new scientist to cook him dinner. I've forgotten what he liked to eat.

Here's what I know. Raw meat. Cold wind. Warm hide.

Five years ago, I walked into an open stand of aspens, peered into a felled log, and the man ceased to matter. From that exact moment, I wrote no new reports to send back to a university, took no video. Since then, it's been all about the wolves, all eyes and ears and tails, and the alpha bitch holds my best focus with her stamina, dominance, strength. I stare at the brown fur behind her ears.

I look into her timeless amber eyes.

I've watched her mate with the alpha male and give birth to many litters of cubs, which stay a year or two then leave. In the pack, the alpha male gives power to her with every new act of birth.

Others in the pack interest me, but she is the fascination point. There's a mystery in her face, in the lighter pelage tones at her throat, in her fangs, something closer speculation does not erase. Since I got here, I've watched her chase off beta bitches who try to breed with the alpha male and bite the omega wolf shamelessly when he irks her. I've seen her pick the pack's kill many times and disable the prey. She's taken down so many elk and deer that if there were a count to show her conquests, it would seem some several herd.

Though I don't participate in hunts, I'm their daily watcher. On days with kills, first, the pack scatters any assembled animals and watches them disperse. This appears a game of sorts, an unmotivated attack from many sides, but it's really a structured weeding. The pack seeks the creatures the herd can do without, the straggler they will attack *en masse*, killing surplus only sometimes, if the time is ripe, if the mood is particularly hostile or feral.

My alpha bitch decides. When she chooses a mark, her ears perk up, her eyes zero in, her tail moves to the left. She lopes and signals, so the pack closes in. She can't be more than eighty-five pounds, but fierce isn't quantified in size. Among them, her ferocity is unquestioned.

Hunt performance makes the status of each member, which is why I'm only peripheral, which is why I watch her so closely. As long as she doesn't reject me, the other wolves can't. Usually, the pack chases the animal until it reaches exhaustion—mainly ungulates. When the chosen animal collapses or can hardly stand, they pounce and gnaw off hunks of flesh until it dies.

Feasting keeps them vigilant, alert. After the alphas take first taste, they offer the betas and sometimes the omega a share. Though she is generous, I never think of eating what the alpha bitch offers. I don't share the hunt. Even so, on a good day, I imagine I am one of her pups, grown enough to get my own provisions, still a favorite, not a threat. Accepted. I don't imagine I'm an auntie wolf, one of the lesser females that lactates and shares the nursing of the young. I don't imagine I'm a cub-sitter beta male, or even the omega wolf that the rest harass when times are bad.

When I regard the alpha bitch, I'm just like a malformed, weaker child who wants only her proximity and acceptance. Beside her, all bad memories dissociate. If she is my spirit animal, she is fine and ruthless and strong. Beside her, I feel no winter cold, accommodate springs and summers even easier.

In these five years I've known her, we've rarely encountered humans, but this changes now, since the pack moves more frequently. The male alpha seeks constant higher ground, senses more disturbance. He's not wrong.

With my human eyes, I see more men's trappings in the woods. With my human ears, I hear them talk. Hunters. When they banter, it's about saving elk or breaking laws. It's about extermination of wolves, permits or no permits.

"The wolf is the devil," I hear a father tell his son. "It eats livestock and peoples' dogs. Let's kill as many as we can. Wolves are taking over this valley, the whole area. Pretty soon they're going to kill us all. They won't stop at elk. Shoot those sonofabitches! Shoot them all!" He and his son have rifles. Their voices echo and carry.

"The one right there?" the son asks. The boy is only eight.

"Yeah! That one. The light one with the violet gland!"

My pack senses but is uninterested in either of them until a shot rings out through the trees, missing a nearby beta.

"Close," the father says. "Aim again."

The alpha male takes the next missed shot as his cue to alert the pack to depart, and we dart deeper into the trees, roam farther that day than the day before. The Alpha Male leads like a disappearing, reappearing totem between the trees, silent and fast. His bitch follows. We all follow.

But encroaching worry occurs as more human exchanges transpire. The betas hound the omega relentlessly. The alpha bitch howls erratically, with eerie tones.

In recent weeks, more bullets enter the air. Nearby. Far away. Sprays of them. Sometimes now, we see wolf corpses, left to rot in the snow.

When I see the carnage left behind, I imagine the shooters must have hefted up the carcasses and took a snapshot as a memoir, photographed themselves with the dead wolves before abandoning the corpses. Hunter selfies.

Their voices resonate. "These fuckers here are huge!" I hear one hunter say to another. "Big and fat. Look at these tracks! Bet those massive ones online could easily have been Idaho wolves by now, the ones mixed with grays come from Canada."

"Somebody posted those shots on the web to rile us up," his partner says. "But I know those pictures weren't taken here. It's Idaho. We got potatoes, not much else. Massive wolves of Idaho? Malarkey. Wolves here are small enough—there's just too many. They're killing all our game. If it's up to me, I'd just like to make sure my unborn son can hunt elk like we've been hunting for generations. I don't care about preserving bred predators!"

"Nez Pierce wouldn't like to hear you say that," his partner says. "They're wolf-friendly and shit."

"Then it's a good thing they ain't here," he replies. "Besides, fuck 'em."

I don't care for the sloppy look of his clothes or the tone of his voice, but the hunter is right. Elk are sparser. As far as we lope, even the pack finds fewer herds. As time passes in this region, hooved beasts dwindle—and I wonder when the people will find it dire enough to reclaim the rights of hunter kills, but my training as a scientist shows me more than just a prey headcount.

As a result of wolf predation, something more important than herds has returned. Young trees. Stands of willow, cottonwood, and aspen emerge, free to grow, growing, grown tall enough to climb on. Songbirds and beavers return for these habitats.

Still, as time passes, orange hunter jackets flood what used to be natural preserves, and memories of my human time in society rush back as my adopted life with the pack is disturbed. Now, two lives clamor at once in my head.

I remember old arguments, the news and its updates, how I used to listen on a small pocket radio, even out here. Yes, more hunters are here. They are looking to kill wolves. They no longer care about regulations.

Wolves, no longer endangered, are in peril. I find it gross that shooters now use words like "harvests" to describe eliminations of packs, as if killing with bullets and leaving to die was similar to plucking of fruit from a tree, as if someone would eat the produce.

Meanwhile, my pack knows nothing of the debates, and I begin to fear for them with each overheard aspersion. Still, the frosts arrive and end, with no new losses to our group, I feel we've been incredibly lucky. This year's cycles go the same as they did before. When my alpha bitch is ready to breed, I realize its February. The weather finally warms. Green shoots poke through snow. The alpha bitch and the alpha male begin courting, though when I see deep orange spots through the foliage as we lope, I tremble. It's killing season.

When I smell gunpowder or see more wolves on the ground, I cry.

I know now what the others don't, what I can't communicate to the pack, which is that it feel like the time of simply living like wolves in the wild is almost over; the government and civilians will take back almost the whole gift of Idaho's Alberta repopulation. They will do it with steel. I look around me and regret I am tortured with foresight.

Wolves worry about today's hunt, next week's roam. Wolves live in the moment and have much shorter lifespans than humans; they have no memory of what has come before. I envy them their full immersions in the days.

Still, spring comes with all the regular signs and that's a blessing. The alpha bitch bleeds and secretes her sex hormones. The alpha male nears. The two bond, sleeping closer, whining, nibbling at each other; they whip each other's faces with their tails. Their intimacy compels.

The whole time they approach the annual mating, I listen for warnings from the bush. I listen for anything beyond yelps and whimpers from the pack. This month, I don't hear it.

The two keep courting until the male alpha mounts his bitch from behind and their organs swell together so intensely, they are bound, almost fused. He can get off her back and stand by her side without pulling his penis free, leaving it inside her like a bent band. Side by side, as if neck and neck in a race, they wait till the sperm has traveled to her depths, till they can separate without pain. I'm glad when they finally release. Together, they would surely be targets.

Though the pack reacts the same, the recent harvesting makes the wolf pups' arrival the more poignant, I decide as the labor comes in April. Born blind and deaf, small enough to lift like melons in my hands though I don't touch them, I already know some won't survive. One was already born dead, a female. This season, the alpha bitch has borne four males and two bitches, one bitch cold on arrival.

I watched her eat the fetal sack from each pup's head to allow it breath, sever the umbilical cords, and eat the placenta. She was so sad this year about the dead one.

She showed it to each member, carried between her teeth, and then, when she had strength, she buried it in the dirt.

At some level, she carries that sadness with her, even a few months later. Now the pups have grown and can take more than her milk. They are that much larger. I get the sense from the movement of the alpha male that we'll soon want to reach the rendez-vous spot since the pups have almost grown big enough to hunt, but as we enter an open valley, a new threat emerges from the sky.

I hear it before I see it. A helicopter, my old life knowledge clamors. Hide. Run!

A sharpshooter hangs from an open doorway. He takes a shot.

He's gunning for us. I cannot tell the pack what they must do. I don't know which barks or whimpers will work as I intend, or even how to convey what may be coming. In, vain, I howl. I cling to the alpha bitch and shout in her ear, "Get out of here. Run for the trees! Tell them to run for cover!"

She acts as if she can't hear me, and the shooter takes another shot. He's now killed the omega. A beta bitch goes down and the whole pack begins to bark and howl. "It's no good," I say to them. "Run!"

The alpha bitch shepherds her cubs. She approaches injured wolves and sniffs their wounds. The shooter does not stop. Soon, he will hit the alpha male, who has also gone to investigate injured wolves —and then he'll hit the alpha bitch too, with her cubs still following. I imagine we are viewed through magnifying scopes and suddenly, I remember that I might be able to help. If I can get human enough, in a hurry, I can help.

I stand on two feet, like a good idea has finally reached me. I shout up to the helicop-ter, "Stop! These are peaceful wolves. Don't shoot!" and I raise my arms, waving them up and down, but I feel like an imposter because I haven't made these human kinds of motions in so long, nor voiced so many human words,

I don't know who these people in the helicopter are—but I know they are dangerous. I know I must pretend to appease them. I shout more, upward to the sky. I have no idea what I'm saying. It comes out sounding foreign, like jibberish.

The people in the helicopter don't register me. More shots rain down.

The man with the gun aims for the alpha male and I watch him absorb the shot and drop. The other betas are then picked off, so my eyes return to the alpha bitch, who now snarls and stands for combat, her pups around her legs. She looks so fierce; I fiercely love her more. Mother, I think. Mother Wolf of Dreams, may I now help you?

I go to her and there is near silence as I travel through the grass to reach her side, just a whirring of helicopter blades for a few frozen seconds that feel like years. But my human memory rushes back more insistently as I behold her, as I near her, standing before her cubs, in partial crouch.

Wind whistles in my ears and I roam, in my mind, to that moment in the aspens with the log, the exact time when I left human roots to travel with this pack. My memory gets clear.

Within it, the alpha bitch's face peers back at me. I've found her, but by accident, with a litter of cubs in a hollow log. In my mind, she crouches and snarls before lunging at my face. She plunges her claws in my neck, her amber eyes like slits. After she takes a bite from my side, the pack joins her and feasts on my body. My blood enters their veins; my life is joined to theirs.

As I think of this now, it feels like the reason I have followed them, the reason behind reasons. I reel. They have never heard me.

The shooter hits a pup next. More shots rain. I feel awakened and terrified. I look up at the helicopter. I look down at the alpha bitch's remaining litter, and it's like I see the silver bullet that comes for her in slow motion, gliding its way into her side, sliding through thick air like a guided missile.

I throw my body between her body and the bullet, but I realize, in that moment, that I no longer have a body. My arms, if they can still be known as such, are raised in pointless supplication. I howl as I have never howled, half human and half wolf in my sound. The bullet passes through me in a wave of heat and takes her down.

I can do nothing. Another shot lands her skull.

More shots ring amidst the yelping and whimpering of pups. One by one, the pack is exterminated until only wolf corpses litter the landscape, which I now walk among. The bullets cannot touch me.

Where are the massive wolves of Idaho that might have helped us, I wonder to myself, the ones the hunters feared? Would they have saved my puny pack? I don't think so. Even a four-hundred pound wolf, should it exist, could be picked off by a man with a gun from a distance.

And, "You want to know what true terror is?" I want to tell someone then, someone up in the sky who shoots death from a stick without fair exchange. "It's a species that poisons and traps another nearly out of existence, resuscitates it for sport, and then rises to annihilate the same species once again. Terror is knowing a circle of violence won't end. Or maybe it's being the one who knows every beloved nearby has been a victim of capricious slaughter.

Wolves do what wolves do because they follow a pattern as old as the hills, one etched in their blood. They care for their own.

The helicopter leaves, and now I know what, or who, I am, I fly my spirit into the dead body of every down wolf in the pack, one by one—mourning him, mourning her. I think, *Esto Perpetua*, Idaho, *Esto Perpetua*... It will go on and on. Of course I have no one to say this to. Even if I did, no one could hear me, not man nor wolf. And what does it mean, in Italian, in Latin? *Mayest thou endure forever! Let it be eternal.*

I want the wolves to be eternal.

While I'm traveling among bodies, I linger longest inside my Wolf Mother because I still care about her legacy, because she is alpha and she was a queen, because I heard her heart beat nightly and slept in her fur. I pretend now her body has birthed me again, as a ghost, as it did when she first killed me, but this time I exit the lower half of her mutilated carcass like a cub.

I flow through her sinews and bone.

But I have no pack now, I realize. I howl for one. It is agony. There are only corpses all around, so I recognize I'm lone.

THE NORTHEAST

CONNECTICUT ◆ MELON HEADS

HOME SCHOOL EXCURSION

HOME SCHOOL EXCURSION

Meg Tuite

"Melonheads are small in stature, frail looking, with long spindly arms and fingers. Their teeth are crooked, blocky, and discolored. Their most conspicuous feature, their heads, are bald and bulbous and out of proportion with their stooped torsos. Some observers say their eyes are red and they glow in the dark."

- Mark Sceurman and Mark Moran, *Weird New England*

Mom tried to drown me in 'Lewis Gut,' the Great Salt Marsh, just once. It was the only time she ever took me out of the house. It was migration season, hundreds of bird-watchers out with cameras on tripods, waiting to capture the flight of kestrels and ospreys. A mother dousing a monstrous head with spindly appendages into the ethereal waves was not sightseeing these folk planned to photograph. She took me at night when I was three.

You think with a cranium the size of a globe, I'd dump like cement, but I floated and a faint green glow cast off of my skin. Mom gripped me in her arms, screamed about God and the devil. At least that's what Dad said. How would I know? I was a vague sense of a being at the time, never photographed. The only childhood memories after that were captured from Mom's lips. Dad left for work on a Wednesday. I was seven. That was our last sighting.

"Heal the sick, raise the dead, cleanse the lepers, cast out demons," a chinless lady with moles scattered across her face like roaches in a kitchen hisses as a group of women surround me, lay their hands on my mountain of a skull. Mom doesn't go to doctors. She is a Christian Scientist. Instead, my head is covered with fingerprints from clammy, misshapen ladies with the stench of clogged drains on their breath translating their disgust into an abstract painting on my scalp. I despised myself and church at an early age.

Cilia, my sister, also carnivalizes me. She takes quarters every Saturday for jostling me in front of her friends. My engorged head bobbles as she lets them trace the blue veins that cascade beneath my cranium. They call me 'Melonhead' until Mom comes home early and finds a line outside our front door.

"What is this? A goddamn parade?"

Cilia gets smacked and the cash is relinquished to Mom's church.

But Cilia wraps me in a world of sound and rhythm like the cleft of a moon. I clasp her tight to my chest, absorbing her throat wavering piano scales, flutes as high as an attic, oboes bulldozing the dust in my closeted life and whole orchestras scratching Bach and Mozart from her record player. She lets me fall asleep in her room to music. My glowing green body is a soft nightlight.

Cilia is invested in proving that poverty doesn't exist in our house. She gets a job as a clerk at Harper's Department Store after school and weekends, cleans up by putting out a bag each week of stolen clothes, make-up, and jewelry with the garbage before closing and, Crazy, her girlfriend with a car, picks up in the alley.

I'm home-schooled. I sit at the kitchen table with my head and neck enclosed in a brace that keep my skull upright and read through encyclopedias and books donated from Stratford High. I discover the word 'masturbate'. The idea of self-pleasure inhabits my thoughts until I get Cilia alone to explain the logistics. I start experimenting. It is a catalyst for seizures embedded with the smell of Mom's potato stew, which was on the stove steeping the first time I jacked off. I waver up and down in cascading waves of receptors.

We live off of Velvet Street, which Cilia always complains is hell to get in and out of because it's down a long hill before one steps foot on to the actual road. I never go out. I sit off to the side of the back screen door. Mom doesn't want any of the neighbors to see that she has bred a demon, even if she does kiss me each night and tell me God has a special plan for me.

Cilia takes photographs of each season on Velvet Street and tacks them up in my room so they are eye-level with my wheelchair, donated by the church. Masturbation becomes a much more delicate operation to perform in the chair. It cuts that activity down by at least a third.

Winter photos are skeletal outlines of branches draped with snow and icicles. Spring holds green tight to its chest and shoots of color peek out of the foliage. Summer and Fall are monstrous. Strange rainbows flame and erupt, flood Velvet Street. It is a mammoth, leafy extravaganza of maple, oak, hickory, elm trees, and strangled mounds of wild poppies, sunflowers and rose bushes. Reds, yellows and every shade of green slap back at me from the photos. I resemble none of them. I want to be a ratty, gnarly bush of exotic thorns. I want to hurt someone with my beauty.

"Cilia," I yell, "Mozart." Cilia's loyalty scathes me with the distress of deformity masked as magnificence. "Play the "Requiem Mass," please."

"You are not dying. You are a whole, radiant planet," she says.

"Radioactive, you mean." I glow demented green at night, not even seen in the landscape. "Take more photos, Cilia."

I am nine years old when the other Melonheads appear. Mom finds them. Four kids just like me live in our neighborhood and three are wheeled into our house. Rena walks or rather staggers with her head and body tilted to the right. Three girls and a boy. We stare at each other. Gerald, Beatrice, Sandy, and Rena have been meeting for two years. They are not Christian Scientists.

The parents pound their fists on the kitchen table screeching about 'Raybestos.' There is an industrial plant, "Raymark Industries," that dumps toxins and pollutes Stratford water and air. I hear the words 'lead', 'asbestos', 'hazardous waste', 'contamination', 'hydrocephalus', and 'I'll sue their ass'.

Mom screams along with them about the contaminated residential area and fighting the EPA, but she has already marked my disease as a personal affront between her and God. I don't think their sword is ever pulled out in public, but at least the parents have something to talk about.

Beatrice answers in a shrill, high-pitched cry. Gerald throws up at least once every time we meet and wears dark sunglasses. Sandy has seizures more than the rest of us, and Rena lashes out and hits. But we have one ability in common that we don't share with anyone else. We can communicate without speech.

"We got things to say," Beatrice lifts her hooded eyes.

"Rena was the first one to talk to me," Gerald twitches. *"She said what you looking at? Then socked me. She leaves a psychedelic bruise."*

"You got a holy hell of a mind," Sandy says. *"You got dancing and songs, makes me sick, all that racket."*

I don't have to look at anyone in particular. I just start thinking questions and their responses are in my head.

"Do you go out?" I ask.

"Brief elasticity. Roll out of houses into cars and back into houses."

"You seen Velvet Street?" I ask the group. Mom's idea of fresh air is setting me up for hours behind the back screen door. The view is a massive rhododendron hedge.

"From car windows. It's hemorrhaging right now."

I point to my photos. *"Summer."*

They agree.

"You know Mozart?"

"That guy playing in your head is hard to miss. He likes to mix his crashes with pounding piano and dilating flutes."

"Yeah, I love him. And I love you," I say.

"Our skulls are expansive. More room for love."

In between seizures, screeches, peeing and vomiting, parents try to teach us the alphabet or feed us. Adult voices are barely a cough. Nothing obstructs our dialogue. These kids aren't reading Shakespeare and anatomy books like me, but they don't say stupid things when we have private talks.

When Cilia comes home she has to lie on her bed for a long while after seeing the other Melonheads. She cries.

"I love Cilia. She's always loved me," I say.

"Our love is incontinent."

"I have two brothers," says Rena. *"They bloom in my blood."*

"My mom is severe and her church is retarded." I make it clear that I am in opposition.

"Rules lull people. We are a mess; disturb routine. Our latches are loose."

The group starts to glow.

Parents come in to my room speaking in sing-song baby voices as they put hoods over their kid's heads, cover them in blankets.

It is humid. At least 90 degrees inside and out.

"When you coming back?" I ask.

"We'll hear you, Mozart," they respond.

Rena pummels her dad as he leads her out. Cilia sits up and gets another look as the posse are carried, rolled and dumped into cars. Mom calls them heathens and goes on about what dirty hippies they are, but she hugs me with tears flaking the corners of her eyes. "You have family," she says.

Cilia comes into my room one night, clutches and rocks me in a stupor for hours. Three boys from school attacked her and Crazy after a party. She keeps chanting their names: 'Thomkins," "Kendall," "Haskins," until they are imprinted like the church hags' fingerprints on my skull.

Cilia is bleeding, her clothes torn and she stinks of sweat and whiskey, but tells me not to say a word to Mom. I seize in her arms. I can't control it. She holds me until I stop flailing, then carries me to her room, puts on "Requiem For a Mass."

I wake up alone in Cilia's bed with the shower running in the bathroom. My head is propped on three pillows. I can't tell what time it is. The blinds are closed.

I meet the Melonheads every Tuesday. Mom still won't let me go out. They take turns meeting at each other's houses. Cilia says Crazy can drive us, but Mom scuffs our brains with nonsensical liturgies.

"They can come here if they want to be educated. Those hippies got no idea about Jesus or prayer. They keep talking about this doctor and that. Hasn't helped any of their dirty, whining brats? I don't see any head shrinkage. At least we've got the Word of the Lord in this house. Now, let's pray."

Every Tuesday the King Jame's Bible waves up at them from the middle of the table.

Beatrice, Gerald, Sandy and Rena are my blood, heart, legs and eyes. I am Mozart. I can talk to them whenever I want.

"Do people ever see you?" I ask.

"Savage faces stare out from car windows. Doctors write about our eyes retracting, turning downwards, call it a symptom. We choose not to look back."

"Do you sneak out at night?"

"What do you call this?"

They are right. This is a form of deceit. No one else knows we communicate.

"No. I mean bodies and all." They are imagining what it would be like.

It is a full moon. Cilia uses the word, 'hallucinatory,' to represent the night. I can't speak. Every pore on my skin inhales the fat, wet air of Velvet Street. Deciduous crowns taper mumbling trees swaying overhead. Owls, coyotes, hawks, creatures caw, screech, hoot, howl, but I can't look up, just out, ahead at vagrant light that scatters through the woodland and the rustling breath of life everywhere.

Haskins is driving. "It pains me to look at you."

"I'm not the road, asshole. That yellow line? Try to stay on the right side of it. Cops are everywhere," Thomkins says. "Now, what was I telling you?"

"That your stupid ass might get a football scholarship," says Kendall.

"Yeah. I guess I'm not the moron in this conversation after all. Beer, please?" Mike lifts a beer from the slush-iced cooler, cracks it open and hands it up.

"Well, I've got something that just might interest you losers."

"You finally paying for gas, cheap bastard?" Haskins asks.

"Even better. I got my hands on some Rufies."

"Roofy? One of those tripping drugs? I'm not up for that shit," Thomkins says. "I like to be in control."

"Thank God you can play football, you dimwit. It's the rape drug. Pick a girl. Put one in her drink and you've made your touchdown."

"Are either of you idiots keeping track of where we are? I'm the driver, not the navigator. And can someone hand the captain up here a beer?" asks Haskins.
Mike opens another Bud and hands it forward.

"Velvet Street is up on your left. Can't remember how many streets," says Kendall. "And it's a dirt road, so no yellow line."

Haskins glares back at three guys in the back seat. "Who are you guys, anyway?"

"That's Redmond and Mike, right?" They nod. "They know the girl who's having the party and bought the beer you're drinking, cheapass. What's her name?"

"Rena," they both answer.

"Rufies, you say? Nice job. How many you got?" Haskins asks.

"Enough for each of us to hypnotize some virginal snatch into the bushes."

Beers are slurped.

"Here's Velvet. Okay, boys, let me just say that these girls are glowing hot," says Mike. All heads tilt back in unison as they chug down the last of the beer.

Thomkins tosses his empty out the window, rubs his hands together. "I'm getting at least two girls tonight."

Haskins laughs. "Maybe we can swap."

Crazy got her nickname when she was just nine and slid a knife out from under her pillow and threatened her dad. That knife kept her alive and potentially lethal, until she dropped lunacy one night into a vague halo of heroin she sucked into her lungs and grain alcohol mixed with Kool-Aid. One minute she was surrounded by familiar, animated faces inhaling pot and sipping booze at a party and next she was crawling through bloody grass and leaves while Thomkins, Kendall, and Haskins were the jagged landscape, an artillery of dicks and crooning, defiling tongues of fire. She heard Cilia detonating fury through the frontline like a gun with a silencer.

Velvet Street is dusty, murky and framed by high sagging trees that have the moon slithering in and out like someone flickering a flashlight on and off.

"What's the address, Mike?"

"3347. Up ahead on the left."

The car juts forward, hits something and stalls.

"What the hell was that?"

"It's a goddamn tree in the road."

They pile out of the car. The headlights are out.

Haskins kicks the front tire. "I got a fucking flat."

"You got a spare?"

"Was going to fix it when I got some cash."

"How about a flashlight?"

Haskins rummages though his glove compartment.

"Let's just walk to the party, deal with this later."

"Creepy out here." Haskins waves the flashlight up over the trees and sticks it under his chin, howls.

Cilia howls back.

"Who was that? Kendall, shut the..."

Rena, Gerald, Beatrice, Sandy and I are rolled out in red wagons tied together. Mike's idea. He and Redmond are Rena's brothers. Crazy babysits the Melonheads for lots of cash. The parents barely get out at night before Crazy inhabits their homes like a soft candle. Mike and Redmond will do anything for her. She is a quiet, dark necessity, blessed with petty crime and an affinity for the abnormal. Girls at school call her psychotic, but never to her face. She dyes her hair blue and moves her purple lips in a silent chant when she walks the halls.

We glow gothic green in the thick-caked walls of the forest. Our heads are hydrocephalic balloons attached to alien bodies, a holiday parade.

"We got other powers," Rena's eyes glow red. *"Never got to practice except on each other and Gerald's cat, Doodle. Your eyes are already red, Mozart. Anger does it."*

I could see three guys ahead of me, whimpering and pleading, with their arms dead at their sides.

"Why don't they run?" I ask.

"Because we paralyzed them," Beatrice says.

"What?" I ask. *"How the hell do you do it and why didn't you tell me?"*

"It really works," says Rena. *"Look at them."*

Thomkins, Kendall, and Haskins appear hypnotized by our eyes.

"How?" I ask.

"Ever heard of Rufies?" Rena asks. *"Mike slipped one in their beer before they got here. It can cause potent amnesia, but together our brain power can paralyze them, and they won't forget us."*

The mind can pack a vision journey of freckled light kissing tops of alpines, a mosquito's proboscis piercing its host, the fingered pulse of gust sweeping over skin, without ever leaving the house. Someone has listened, whether God or the devil. I am a dangerous destination. I am the haunting whisper of the choir in Mozart's "Requiem Mass." I start humming it and soon all of us are.

Mike shoves the three guys in the back seat of their car.

Cilia wheels us to the car. Redmond lifts us into the back seat. The door shuts.

We are piled on top of the rapists. If we are toxic, then they are waste. Beatrice vomits. Gerald spasms in a seizure, convulsing and contracting over the three tremulous teenagers. Rena swats everyone. It is a kaleidoscope of motion, pain, rank odor, and wailing.

"Gnaw on them."

"They don't taste like chicken."

"If we're toxic, maybe we can infect them."

Beatrice vomits again.

"Use your teeth. Gouge them."

"What if they have diseases?"

"They are diseases."

Gerald loses a tooth.

Thomkins and Haskins are catatonic when Redmond opens the door and carries us, one by one, and straps us into Crazy's Datsun hidden behind some trees.

Crazy pulls Kendall out of their junked, putrid car and watches him crawl, like she and Cilia did the night they were raped. His movements are snail-like, barely visible in the moonlight. She smacks him facedown in the dirt with her boot. He lays there, hacking.

"Melonheads will find you," she hisses in his ear. "Rapists are especially fragrant."

Crazy takes out her knife and gets in the backseat next to Thomkin's and Haskin's limp bodies. She studies the bite marks on their extremities, then carefully slices the letters **m-e-l-o-n** below each knuckle of their right hands, and **h-e-a-d-s** on the other. She is an artist, has a thing for symmetry.

THE MIDWEST

WISCONSIN 🦔 THE HODAG

The Hodag of Rhinelander, Wisconson

ILLINOIS 🔶 THE TUTTLE BOTTOMS MONSTER

Alfred of Tuttle Bottom
or: My Father's Nose is Corpse Floss –
I've Only a Dash of Blood

MICHIGAN 🦫 THE DOGMAN

Lemon Chest

WYOMING 🔶 THE JACKALOPE

The Killer of Rabbits and Brothers

SOUTH DAKOTA ▬ BANSHEE OF THE BADLANDS

Badlands Serenade

THE HODAG OF RHINELANDER, WISCONSIN

Brian Krans

"The Hodag dates back to 1896 when its creator, a well-known prankster and lumberjack of the Rhinelander area, announced that he had discovered a great, hairy black beast hiding out in the trees around Rice Creek. Gene Shepard made his story a real whopper, describing how he piled rocks in front of the monster's den to trap it and then poking a chloroform-soaked rag inside to knock the creature out."

- Linda S. Godfrey, *Monsters of Wisconsin*

Dead children don't look like dolls.

They often suffer horribly from the hands that are supposed to care for them. Shakings, beatings, it doesn't matter. There's little makeup and mortician care can do to make it look like it was a child's time to die.

No mother ever recovers from seeing her child inside a casket, but Kathryn Mitchell's was fortunate enough to have one. Whatever or whoever attacked her and left her gutted-out body in the ditch along Hwy. 17 at least had the decency to leave her pale face intact. It gutted her out completely.

Kathryn was last seen Thursday, July 9. Her mother had let her walk by herself to her friend's house a block down the road. Within a half hour, the two families and neighbors began searching the nearby woods, but there was no sign of her.

No one heard screams or noticed anyone unusual. None of the neighbors had priors outside the usual handful of OWIs. No registered pedophiles lived within a mile of her home.

Kathryn's body was found in the woods behind her house four days later. There were no defensive wounds. She didn't have a chance to fight back.

Kathryn was the first. Emily Johnston was the second. Nancy Drosdowski was the third.

Their wounds were consistently centered at vital and other internal organs. Their bellies and chest cavities were cleaned down to the bone and one was extracted.

Each girl was missing her lowest rib.

I've been to all their crime scenes, notified all of their families, and attended all of their funerals.

Darla Ostrowski was laid to rest in a blue dress, and I was there looking for the devil himself. With only 7,800 people in town, I was skeptical of every adult in those girls' short lives. The first suspects in a child's death is her parents.

"Thank you for coming," Darla's mother said as I approached the casket. She wore the red and swollen eyes better than most, but she still asked, "Why isn't the person who killed my daughter in jail?"

Because there are no leads or physical evidence, I didn't say.

"He will be soon," I said. "I promise."

The girls' wounds were consistent with those of being attacked by an animal. The DNR confirmed there were no wolves in the area and the Humane Society has dealt with loose dog sightings swiftly.

The girls were plucked from their homes with no signs of forced entry. They'd disappear and return dead and mutilated hours or days later, all without a sign of who was responsible.

The pattern showed true madness, a savage killer on the loose, turning children into mere cavities void of organ or tissue.

Locals began saying the Hodag had returned. It was a local legend created by Eugene Shepard in 1893. He claimed to have killed the horned, fanged, clawed, and spiked-back beast, but it was quickly outed as a farce to sell tickets at the Oneida County Fair.

Their only factual connection is that the Hodag allegedly ate all-white bulldogs and all the recent slayings have been white girls.

Some claimed the Hodag had returned from legend to feast. It ate the nutritious vital organs of the young, suckling the unpoisoned life out of them, all without disturbing their faces.

Teardrops left untouched. Screams left unheard. Childhoods left unfinished.

As 95 percent of Rhinelander is white and the Hodag was 100-percent fiction, our new Hodag was a real predator, not a fable.

I went home after Darla's funeral. The technician was still there, showing Jennifer, my wife, how to set our new security system. That night, and every one after, our five-year-old, Jack, slept in our bed.

There weren't many waking hours dedicated to being with Jack, but everything I did was for him.

✦

Mayor Johnson initially shunned any outside assistance in fears four mutilated children would gain national media attention. The killings were occurring during our busiest tourism season.

He spun the dusk-to-dawn curfew as a public health initiative, dubbed the "The Summer of Sleep."

"Sleep is something we all take for granted," he told The Northwoods River News. "You can take back the night by saying yes to a good night's sleep."

He declined comment on the killings, only fueling further speculation.

Locals didn't take any chances and fled the town with children intact. The only children in Rhinelander belonged to tourists who didn't know there was something out there feeding on them, and that would soon end as well.

The next victim was Chief Schulte's daughter, Tayna. She was eight, the oldest yet, reported missing when her father, my boss, went to wake her in the morning in their house on Newell Street. There was nothing out of the ordinary. She'd vanished from her bedroom and reappeared as a gutted corpse.

"This is too much, David. I have to think of my family," he told me at her funeral. "I'm getting Pam and the boys out of here. You should do the same."

"I would, but someone's got to stop this guy," I said.

"Then do it," he said, "and call me when you do. I want to be the one to put a bullet in his skull."

The next morning, I drove the lead car escorting them out of town. So many other officers had quit and left Rhinelander that RPD couldn't enforce the curfew, let alone any other crime not directly related to dead children.

That's when the news vans descended from afar. Our quiet town turned into a childless media feeding frenzy. That's the last time I remember being able to sleep.

There was nothing Mayor Johnson could do to prevent the media onslaught. We were hoping it would help catch the killer, but all it did was perpetuate the myth of the Hodag.

It only attracted the kind of attention we didn't want.

The sounds of children playing outside until the streetlights come on during long summer nights were replaced by adventure-seeking tourists who'd drink all night, hooting and saluting the moon in hopes they weren't too old for the Hodag to take them. Or at least those are the howling jokes they make as they stagger to their cars to get home.

Despite the killings, many people stayed behind. They had businesses they couldn't afford to close, moves they couldn't afford to make, or a conviction that they'd be the vigilante to stop the Hodag.

As hunters kept their rifles at the ready, anything that rustled a bush at night was flooded with gunfire. Many were firmly convinced they were hunting an animal, not a human monster.

Tips came in regularly from people reporting suspicious behavior, but even with intense questioning none had any merit to them. Every possible suspect had the last two months of their lives dissected and disemboweled like the children of Rhinelander.

All day, I followed up on those tips and spent my nights with files spread all over the kitchen counter as Karen and Jack slept downstairs. I never thought they were in danger. The killer only targeted little girls.

The only additional protection I thought they needed was sparing them the details of the investigation. I put my files away each night before joining them in bed.

But when a beast of prey loses one source of food, it'll quickly go for whatever is available.

🐗

Jordan Jorgensen, age seven, was the first male victim.

Jack Bohn, age five, was the second. It was sometime Tuesday morning in early August. Aug. 8 to be exact.

"Don't you hear it, Daddy?"

I thought I heard it in a dream, but I awoke to the sounds of my wife screaming.

"Jack?! Jack! Where are you?!"

I sprung up and began searching the house. There were no broken windows or pried open doors. The backyard was empty.

I dialed dispatch and had them immediately begin searching. Another Amber Alert was issued. We'd done it a dozen times before, but this was the first time I scoured the area in a T-shirt and underwear.

"Everyone wake up! Jack is missing!" I yelled as I ran through the streets.

I'd been investigating missing children for months and was no closer to finding the killing since I began.

The two available squad cars responded in minutes, their spotlights lighting up any dark corner in our neighborhood.

"David, what are you going to do?" Jennifer asked, panic and fear surging through her face.

We staked out the backyard, waiting for Jack's killer to return his body. We waited, Jennifer becoming more despondent with each hour.

I was doing all I could, but I should have sent my family away a long time ago. I should have done more to protect them. I should have taken Chief Schulte's advice and left when he did. But I wanted to catch the killer.

Jennifer committed suicide three days later after there was still no sign of Jack. She left the car running in the garage with a packed bag in the trunk. It's as if she was planning to run away, but couldn't leave Jack behind.

I was in the backyard, waiting for my son's killer to show his face. I only heard the running engine after it was too late.

Jack's body reappeared in a creek a half a mile from home. Whoever or whatever took him came as close as he could without getting caught. Jack was hollow, but his face was left untouched.

My wife and son were given a joint funeral.

There was barely anyone left in Rhinelander to attend and people from out-of-town were too scared to come.

I don't blame them. I was supposed to solve the case, but I wasted too much time assuming it was human.

Take my advice and leave this town. There's no good reason to stay.

I was born here and I'll die here, but not before I catch the Hodag. It took my son and my wife, taking any reason I had to care about living or dying.

I don't know what it is, but every single time it takes a life, I'll be studying what it's left behind. Someday it will mess up. It may move on, and I'll follow it.

Maybe someday the Hodag will come for me, and I hope it does. I want to look it in the eyes and see what Jack, Darla, Kathryn, and the other children saw before they died.

I want the Hodag to look into my eyes before I kill it. It's not a man, and it's not a beast, but all that concerns me is that it is a killer.

You can come to whatever conclusions you want.

The Hodag—in one form or another—is real.

It could be hunting you right now.

ALFRED OF TUTTLE BOTTOM
OR: MY FATHER'S NOSE IS CORPSE FLOSS – I'VE ONLY A DASH OF BLOOD

Ben Segal

"The Tuttle Bottoms Monster was first reported in the north outskirts of Harrisburg in the section of town referred to as Doris Heights. Hunters and people who would park along the road in that area would make frantic calls to police and sheriff departments reporting a large furry animal that resembled an overgrown anteater."

- Bruce Cline, *More History, Mystery, and Hauntings of Southern Illinois*

My two families are equally and oppositely disgusted. I've got the cat tied down spread-eagle on the picnic table and have carefully shaved her stomach area. The steak knife and fork are ready, the large checked napkin's tied neatly around my neck, and my father cannot believe what he's seeing. Neither, of course, can Mr. Henderson.

What are you doing with that cat? Scream the two of them in unison.

I should explain. I come from a long-line of disembowelers—my father and his father and his father before him and on back as far as anyone can remember. Here in Tuttle Bottom, I guess you can say we're kind of famous. I was expected to similarly rip through all our human neighbors, was raised for it, trained as boy to kill insects and then small mammals. When I grew up, I was to have been taken out to look for people.

But I never really grew. Or I grew a little and then stopped and only grew wider. I ended up a few feet tall, stubby and hose-nosed and, worst of all, with a face far more goofy than terrifying.

Each morning, my brothers would come home with stories of the hunt, of sinking snouts feet-deep in the bored-out chest cavities of lost hikers and off duty park rangers. They bragged of slurping innards in the backs of Chevrolets, of gut-covered good-times in rusted Impalas, nosefuls of flesh by the wrong lover's lanes. They told of a feeling I could never grasp: the wet sensation of a nose wriggling through a fresh throat-hole, scraping gently past the teeth of a wide dead mouth.

I could only catch crawdads, the odd gopher. I learned to tell jokes and hunt for my little meals and basically strive for a life in which I was a the softest-possible disappointment to everyone around me. My father and brothers, you can well imagine, teased me mercilessly. Eventually I could no longer take the ridicule and I left our swamp community for what I imagined would be a lonely life of rat-killing and hermitage.

The problem with my plan was that I wandered, accidentally, into a suburban neighborhood and fell through a soft patch in the garage roof over which I was chasing a small raccoon. Mr. Henderson, the garage's owner, found me cowering between discarded gas cans and was astonished to find I could talk. A little quick thinking on my part led me to offer the explanation that I was a crash-landed alien.

I have to give him credit—Mr. Henderson took the whole situation in stride. I assured him that I was harmless (which, unfortunately, I am) and he kindly allowed me to live with his family. I played Sorry with his children, learned to bake chicken Kiev, was generally welcomed as an offbeat family mascot.

The one problem I had was keeping my hands off the Hendersons' cat. I love eating cats. My whole life I've liked nothing more than the taste of feline tartar. But I knew the Hendersons would throw me out if I ever touched Fluffy, so I let her torture me with her presence and only occassionally snuck out to snack on a stray.

All in all, things were good. I came to feel a real affection for my adopted family. I manned the grill for weekend barbecues, became an avid Bulls fan. I helped Lisa, their oldest daughter, to write her college applications. She was supposed to attend Northwestern in the fall. I'll get to that. But what I want to emphasize is that, for a time at least, I truly became a Henderson.

Unfortunately, no idyll is ever endless. I learned one day that my father had come looking for me. We swamp apes of Tuttle Bottom have both a strong, terrible odor and a tremendous sense of smell. The combination allows us to find each other across miles of rank Illinois bog water. Beyond the marshes, our scents stand out like smell-beacons and I had picked up my father's harsh, distinctive musk circling closer and closer to the Henderson home.

My father is repulsive, but he is not entirely without an ethics. He lives by a perverse code of family and honor, so I always knew he'd think my desertion shameful. Still,

I didn't realize he would come looking for me. I assumed he'd simply write me off as dead. I must have underestimated the embarrassment caused by my departure. The fact that I smelled him coming could mean only that dead-to-him was not enough, that he'd come to finish the job.

Out of consideration for my hosts, I'd been bathing twice daily and regularly dousing my body in a combination of aftershave and perfume. The scent-masking was probably slowing my father down, but I knew he'd find me soon and that, when he did, he would rip open the Hendersons and probably make me eat them before disemboweling me as well.

So I resolved to leave. The Hendersons had been a better family to me than mine ever was and, though I could not escape my fate, at least I could spare them. Depressed and preparing to flee, I began to play a little nose-straw in the Henderson liquor cabinet. And I'm not proud of what happened but I guess I overdid the schnapps because I grabbed Fluffy and stuffed her into my duffel before climbing out the bathroom window.

I guess in that moment I decided that, since I was leaving anyway, I could at least, finally, eat the cat. Pampered housecat has really always been my favorite meal and there's no feline in the midwest so coddled as Fluffy. I stroked her gently through the duffel's canvas and began to trundle off toward the disused picnic area of the neighborhood park.

I

The Hendersons must have followed my footprints—I forget how distinctive they are—and, once I was outside the confusing smell zone of a suburban subdivision, my father easily tracked down my scent. I, meanwhile, had been fixedly fixing Fluffy as my last meal.

Which is how we got to now: the howling cat, the howling fathers. I can read the distain on my real one's face: how I can I possibly prepare to eat a cat when a defenseless human family stands right in front me? And I can similarly read the shock and sadness written across the whole little clan of Hendersons. I look to them and shake my head. "You shouldn't have followed me here."

And they shouldn't have. My father disembowels the lot of them and sets eagerly upon their internal organs. I do the same to the cat. I feel my nose as it slips through Fluffy's body, a small moment of joy before my father moves on to me.

LEMON CHEST

Jamie Grefe

"In 1967, two fishermen were casting lines from a rowboat on Claybank Lake in Manistee County. They were about to head back to shore when one of the anglers noticed an animal swimming in their direction. As it approached the boat, the men were horrified to see the animal paddling with all fours had a humanlike face."

- Sally Barber, *Myths and Mysteries of Michigan*

When Bob, Jack, and Pete hightailed it away from the creature's burning lair and back to Clancy's hunting shack, they were already too late—a flittering fly orgy of innards swirling the shack, rot-body stench, and the gore of nibbled bones, bite marks—their cutthroat once-upon-a-time buddy, still dead on the floor.

But now, not in one piece.

And Bob, the last one to barrel in, left the door wide open, even thought of ditching his pals right then and there, follow the moon's light or some star pattern he couldn't read to a side road, hijack a tree and ascend, or dig a hole, and just wait for the morning sun to make his way home. To never kick a dog again, forevermore keep pockets bulged with treats or squishy toys. Instead, he focused his good ear (the oversized one) to the night forest—a branch snap, perhaps, a rustling swill, leaf shuffle, anything to warn the other two of their pursuer, or to convince himself they didn't see nothing, no, sheriff, not a lick—Indeed, Bob thought, *this* is a night to die.

The shack's woodstove—it was Clancy's, "*was*" being the key word—still bubbled stubby log chunks and beneath the blast of all that spilled blood, Bob inhaled the now-tarred coffee rimming the pot on the stove—made him want to sober up.

Or drink, if drinking would make dawn come quicker.

"Flubberin' Christmas," Bob yelled, cramped by the stink. "He reeks right like—should have dug a grave, boys." He threw a fist at his bulging mouth to siphon the rising vomit that tickled his tongue through the threads of his hands. Didn't help. Gagging and spit-hacking grub, Bob doused the floorboards in bean bits and runny egg yolks, soggy toast and booze, the sound of his retches burbling to the tip of his head; he couldn't hear that nearby *snap-snap-snap* of twigs breaking outside in the night.

Busy-body Jack, was already shivering, clawing through Clancy's closet in the back room, clattering shotgun shells all over the floor like a flabby juggler at an arthritic circus.

If only Bob could tell those Jack bullets wouldn't work. Not on what was coming.

But Bob didn't know that yet.

Next came the hard slap of Pete slip-smacking on the linoleum, trying to bat the flies up to the bare light bulb on the ceiling or at least direct them away from Clancy's ripped-to-shreds corpse—spotty specks of flannel, jean tatters, soiled meat, skin piles scattered. Clancy (chunks of him) stuck to and hung from everything in that busted-up kitchen. Half his old head grinning toothless in a Crockpot. Legs with no feet. Fingers with scraped knuckles, nails missing. And his blood made the kitchen table shiny like caramel apple eyeballs.

"Close the goddammned door," Jack said, twisting past Bob's puke splotch, quick-shoving Bob to the sofa, slamming the shack's front door, and jimmying the latch into place with a bolt. "You want to keep spitting up timbers or you want me to change your Pampers, Bob?"

Bob groaned, hefted himself off the spring-sprung sofa, mouth drooping anger, and threw a punch at Jack. He missed, skidded on his gut-paste, and nailed his left knee hard. "Help me up, you cocksucker," he said. "I ain't the one who thought it would be funny to torch that mutt's hut—probably still smoking, those timbers," but Jack burst out a tight laugh in two bursts, and strode past to the crapper.

Pete, back on his feet, belched his authority, shuffled out of the kitchen with a meat cleaver the size of a Ford, swung it around like he knew how to use it. He nodded Bob toward the fire poker. He wiggled his eyebrows. "Arm up," he said.

"What?" Bob said. "That thing?" tugging up his Dickies, tossing off his denim coat and hissing out a string of slurred nasties. "You all get to play butcher, give me a limp stick, well ain't this *poupon* on a pickle."

Pete: "We gonna show Lassie something, sure enough."

The toilet flushed, door kicked open loud. Bob and Pete yelped at the sound, forgetting all about Jack and when Jack groaned out, gripping his overhung gut, they shook their heads in disapproval. Fat Jack had slicked back his stringy grey mane, and looked close to a weathered gump-balloon on a cougar hunt.

But there was nowhere to run. The nearest town was miles and miles too far—and impossible to navigate the trails on broken bottles of shine and a gutted motor, unfixable.

"And wasn't me, Bob, you prick," Pete said. "How was I supposed to know we were burning down the house of the Devil himself—beaver-houses, shit-shack, deer-hotels all over the woods—*amIright?*—and you think you've been around the bush, ain't no dog I never seen."

Flustered and beaten, Bob was done listening, coughed, and pulled out a wrinkled pack of smokes. He hit the lighter, then took a drag, spat. He thought about summer drinks, carburetors and Marcy, Johnny Lee, and the old Elk Tavern Boys out on Hubbard Lake making lemons out of orange juice. If he sucked on that smoke hard enough, he could disappear inside himself, melt through the cedars, undo all this dumb damage done, just in time for Marge to tip the tap, tap the foam off the top, and put it on his tab. Could drink the American dream clean.

Almost.

Jack huffed, pulled the shotgun to his chest, hobbled across the room, and peeled back a curtain.

Pete took one step toward Jack, stopped scared, legs stiff, cleaver at the ready.

Bob grabbed the fire poker. The spent logs were still a bed of orange warmth. He squatted down and tried to soak some of that heat into his lungs like how he sucked his cigarette. He blew a cloud of smoke into the stove, but he wasn't a God-fearing man, not since his Judy's lawnmower accident splattered his pastoral lawn gut-red-death-red. At this venture in the game, though, any proverbial wave of the wand under the sun would help. Flick a bit of ash, blood of a toad, a few gold coins stuffed in his socks, and stir the honey pot before that nightmare—slobbering-dog-beast-wolf-wendigo-of-a-what-used-to-be-a-man—came pawing for retribution for what was done to his stick-figure abode. Abode...shit-sauce, it was a teepee of rotten logs, some doo-rags, and a clump of old pizza boxes for a bed. Not even half a mile from their shack. Private land, my ass. Screw this weekend in the middle of northern nowhere.

And Jack and Pete saw surprises, too, had seen those bone-bodies stuffed in a pit, arms pinned through branches, others spread-eagled, and more bodies all done up properly seated like a little girl's pretty party complete with the tea cups and plastic plates as if that beast had a sense of humor.

And Clancy, dolt dead-on-the-floor Clancy shouldn't have lipped, sent them out for a walk—the fool.

Some fools need to be nipped—how Clancy came running in mad at dusk, all hopped up on gasoline huffs and a lungful of those pills he said his hotshot brother gave him. Clancy's disrespecting tongue wasn't nothing but trouble for these old "Sag-nasty" vets, wildcat-drinkers who done drunk, got drunk, drank-drunk, and drunk more. That's when Bob pinned slobbering Clancy down, but what he didn't do was slice the rhubarb when it came time to skinning neck-jerky. Slitting Clancy's throat was all Jack and Pete, let truth be told.

Bob burped away the memory, Clancy's murder, and dropped his cigarette in the stove, watched the butt turn into a burnt flower.

Pete bent down, real close to Bob's ear: "I can feel that dog coming," he said. "Sniffing us out."

Bob, big ears perking, pushing at his good one, could hear something close out by the car. And Jack, still granny-peeking out into the darkening dark, he was leaning way to close to the glass and when those monstrous claws—fuzzy paws, fat-fingered, razor fingernails like train spikes—smashed through the window; it was too late.

Bob hollered, wobbled to his feet, and ran, plowing into Pete, sending the shotgun blasting out a chunk of wood. He dove to a semblance of safety behind the sofa, just in time to watch Jack's wrinkled skin-sauce crumple. Those claws dug right through his face, bottle-capped his head clean off his neck. Jack's body danced backward, back into the cabin, dropped his shotgun on the floor, chicken-hopped, spun in a few blood-sputtering circles, and strutted headless toward the kitchen. His dead feet mucked in a clump of Bob's puke pool and slid to a fountaining end of drizzled farts and twitches, thus drizzling the kitchen redder with his death.

And Bob looked up from the sofa, turned to the window—not to Pete, fear-frozen and chattering right next to him—and just about wet his corduroys at the unholy sight of that... Dogman.

The Dogman, absolutely, no other way to say it.

This beast, hovering just outside the window, Bob saw so clearly, was actually hunched over like he'd grown taller since they last saw him in the woods, but that was through the smoke of his torched abode. Black-grey fur. Crusty red eyes. Muzzle mid-snarl. Those fangs, tongue sagging, all lit reddish in the blood-tinged light of the shack. Bob looked right at the sucker, didn't even realize the sucker was looking right at him, unblinking at his soul, and the room slowed, so slow you could have thought hours or nights upon still nights had passed. The Dogman thumped his claw down on the windowsill and held it there tight with Jack's sick blood raining in gross trails down the wall to the floor.

And Dogman—as if to mimic Bob—made this gulping wheeze, and in three gulps, he vomited up Jack's torn-off face and head-bones, sent his mangled remains shooting across the room, smack-blathers into Pete's flabby chest.

Pete scrambled, picked up, fired the shotgun at the Dogman, blasted him back from that shattered window and Bob swore he heard a yelping whine rise, gravelly and wet.

"Jack!" Pete said, cleaverless now, but gung-ho ready to fire, staring at the black hole where the Dogman just was, and said: "Gotcha, you dumb-dog sonofamutt—you see that, Bob, a dog, saw—oh, mercy, that shot, got him good."

Bob used the fire poker like a cane and stood. And this might be his chance to run. He could do it, just keep that good ear against the wind, and cast those sails home, old man. But no, now Pete had that shotgun aimed at Bob's head, barrel shaking. Pete's arms jiggled scared. "Sorry, Bob, but dammit if you ain't gonna take the fall first."

"You don't want to do this," Bob said. He tightened his grip on the fire poker. "We can make right, shoot his head off—it'll be legendary." Bob was scrambling to think his way out of this, had always been a talker in times of trouble. "Lop off its bitch muzzle and tell everyone what he did to Clancy, and the paper—Marty knows someone—this is international. Big, Pete, just don't shoot."

"Ain't no one gonna believe us, Bob."

"Ain't no one have to believe us."

"Why's that?"

"The head," Bob said. "Imagine you taxiderm, mount that canine's cranium there in the garage right next to that six-pointer from last year. This is prime rib, Pete."

"Prime rib ain't watching your friend get his face sucked off."

"We gotta shoot the dog," Bob said. "No other—hell, I'll carve him up myself, give him a poke."

Pete shook his head, wasn't buying it. "Sorry, Bob, but—"

Just then they heard the long howl brew.

This howl was more than a normal dog's howl, was a vibration that raged louder like it was singing itself up from the back of the shack, swirling all around them, just kept building and building higher.

Bob stared at Pete.

Pete tried not to scream his head off from the dizzying layers of dog sounds, but Bob's ears were already humming and his good ear, yeah, well, all the pus that'd built up inside it over the years acted like a shield, thank you, blessed crud. "Pete?" Bob said. "Pete, your damn ears are bleeding. Put down the gun."

And so they were. Pete was grinding his teeth so hard, and with the tremor of that howl, Bob guessed he didn't notice the twin streams of blood jutting out his ears, face scrunched in pain.

The front door exploded.

Pete raged, fired the shotgun at Bob, launching Bob off his feet, right into the wood stove—burned his back-end—and head over heels fumbling down the sofa, smacking the ground, and sliding on his own bile, face first.

Bob thought he done died, but didn't feel a prick of pain, not a prick.

And in that moment of moments, he was spliced otherworldly on the front porch with Judy. It was summers ago when Bob was slimmer. He just fired up the lawnmower for her, settled into his hand-woven wicker chair, and lit a fresh smoke to enjoy the afternoon scent of trimmed grass and tobacco blues. It was perfect, but goddamn if two puffs in he didn't hear his honey, Judy, cry out. In a flash she tripped on some pile of dogshit on the lawn, lost her balance, twisted up on the lawnmower and *snip-splat*; blades blended her pretty nose into shrieking headcheese.

But not this moment.

This moment, face mashed to the floor of Clancy's shack, Bob sat on that porch and finished his smoke to the sound of a stupefied Pete being devoured muscle by snarling muscle, slurps and burping bites. But not this moment.

This moment, Bob stood up, stepped off the porch and out to the edge of the lawn just as Judy hit the switch to turn off the lawnmower, and Mother of Shiva, she was gorgeous—wavy blonde hair all poofy, those Fashion Shack jeans, and her chest-hugging checkered shirt smelled like grass and muff-buttered sweat.

And in this moment, Bob wrapped his arms around her and gave his wife the biggest, warmest hug a husband could ever give.

Just like it should have been, smack dab on this most perfect—

But Dogman wrenched Bob up by the collar and threw him across the room, made the world spin black circles.

Bob opened his eyes to the sight of a blood-painting: Pete's body smeared all over—like how Clancy was in the kitchen—and that shotgun somehow lying right at Bob's feet, right next to the fire poker, but Bob smelled blood, couldn't move right.

And Bob saw the hideous grin of a gaping mouth melded into a dog's head, and the sour waves of power wafting from his majestically hulking frame—part canine, part warrior. And it looked like the Dogman was wearing jeans, some kind of ripped up T-shirt, all brown and fur-stuffed and Bob swallowed the bile in his mouth. He didn't want to run no more. Bob relaxed, went limp. It was the most relaxed he'd been all night. It was like the end, like just beyond whatever otherworldly violence the Dogman had in store for him, was Judy. Beautiful Judy. He could see her standing straight postured and shimmering behind the Dogman, a tall glass of lemonade in her hand, sipping off the top, the kind of lemonade she mixed just to see him pucker. To welcome him into her arms.

And from the back room of the shack, another Dogman—or Dogwoman, for this one had a long river of fur hanging parted from the top of her head—stepped out into the light of the woodstove. Bob's pack of smokes lied on the ground at her feet. The Dogman turned to his Dogwoman and growled, groaned, and shot a stare back to Bob. Bob eased himself up against the wall and looked away.

But the Dogwoman kicked Bob's smokes across the floor. He heard them skid. They hit his boots. He looked up at the two of them. Dogwoman had bloody hair clumps and a pancake slice of Clancy's face clamped between her teeth the way his neighbor's dog used to hold a tennis ball for hours and beg to play. Keeping it safe. Being fully present. "You, you, you wanna play?" Bob said, glancing back at his beautiful not-dead Judy behind the both of them. She sipped that lemonade. And she smiled when Bob asked, gave him a wink.

The Dogman tensed, his whole body suddenly rigid and sniffing, but the Dogwoman made this weird growl-cry, all light and airy, and pulled that splotch of Clancy's face from her mouth. She tossed it to Bob who caught it and, with nowhere to go, squished it into a ball.

Each squeeze smelled of cut grass. "If this don't make it right..." Bob said. "Shit, I deserve worse and you know it." And Bob tossed that skin-ball toward the both of them. The Dogman lunged and caught the sucker, and suddenly a stupid dog-smile sparked on his face.

Bob pulled a lighter from his pocket, held it in his hand.

Dogman mouth-flung the skin-ball to his Dogwoman and she caught it.

Bob struck the lighter and it lit, two tails wagging there in the shack, heads cocked in confusion.

And that skin-ball hit his boots. Again, he tossed the ball to the waiting mouth.

Judy nodded from the background and smiled to Bob, invisibly wonderful.

And outside, somewhere, Bob heard a lawnmower, but the woods near the shack were bright orange now as if the fire from the Dogman's abode had followed the Dogman to the shack.

And it did.

"This is me lying down," Bob said. "This is me lying down."

And with those words, Bob held the flame to his bloody chest and lit his shirt on fire. And it smelled like that tarred coffee from the kitchen, coffee he now knew Judy had put on just for him.

The Dogman dropped the ball from his mouth to his hand, tossed the ball back to Bob one last time.

Bob felt the searing heat of fire drift up his chest and he tucked his legs into each other like he saw those yoga moms do at the downtown rec center.

Fire spread, Bob's skin melting over his charred screams; the smell intensified around him.

And the dog monsters were gone, like that.

Or maybe they were too close and the vivid hotness of the world was just how their eyes looked hovering over him, hungry, jaws wide, too wide, wide enough to chomp into flame-broiled Bob's melted head and tear his weathered skin to giblets.

That cleaver was clutched tight in bloody paws.

It didn't matter, though.

The shack was on fire.

And by the time it did matter, Bob's soft eyeballs were already being paw-spooned out of his head in two squishy smoky *pops*, ears ripped from his smoldering skull and swallowed, smacked, and that lemonade inside his chest—gallons and gallons of sweet ever after—was better than any hunting trip Bob had ever been on.

It was like coming home. To an empty house.

THE KILLER OF RABBITS AND BROTHERS

Natanya Ann Pulley

"Looking for answers to these types of questions is like hunting for Jackalope: you'll never bag one because they don't exist; you may find them, however, when they're ready to present themselves to you."

- David M. Hancock, *Jackalope Hunting*

Linnea's rabbit is dead.

Not the dead of her grandmother that meant she had become invisible. Not the dead of her drowned brother Brad that kept her mother too exhausted to continue weeping. It is the dead of things stiff and blood-streaked and plain as day. She pokes at Bunny several more times with the stick and only manages to bother the surrounding flies for a second or two before they land and lift off the mangled flesh busy and pleased.

Linnea knows what it is like for her family to get bad news. She knows they will fall into their seats and beds and when they move it is only to shift the objects around them from one place to another. To hand off the daily makings of a life. Her family talks in words that no longer hold anything but thuds and whimpers. To receive bad news, to know of the dead, means to live under an awfulness. And 7-year-old Linnea will not be a harbinger of awfulness today. At least, not to her dear mom and dad.

The truth is Bunny had also seemed to be in what was called "mourning" around the house. Brad, who was sometimes loud, rowdy, and a little cruel with Linnea's other possessions, was gentle always with Bunny. Even talked to her a bit with a softness Linnea rarely heard. Until, of course, the group of boys showed up and taunted him out of her world and into another of consuming all the contents of the fridge, smelling of bodies and stuffed heat, and the pushing, shoving of one another out the door. They could never just walk along together, but created a sequence of action and reaction. And loudness. The silence that followed them was a welcome emptying out of time and space, until Brad's death when the empty time and space was all the family knew.

Linnea leans closer to Bunny to inspect its one open eye. The wide darkness it once held seems as dull as its fur. Not matted and bloody, but as if a great smudge was left inside it. Bunny wouldn't mind Linnea's careful inspection of her body. Many afternoons were spent with Bunny as patient, as baby, as detective companion. Linnea knows the weight and dimensions of her rabbit. She knows the bumps and plump bits. And Linnea detects a crushing of sorts had happened. As Linnea moves the fur around with small sticks and even a flat rock, she can see most of Bunny is still there. Not eaten. No puncture marks. Instead, where a roundness in Bunny should be, there is just a sunkenness and the blood from some sort of blunt pounding. And in bubbles around the mouth. It isn't unlike Linnea to notice such things, having lived on a ranch and never being shooed away from all acts of nature and man. And rowdy boys.

One might say after burying the body of Bunny, Linnea sits quietly against a great cottonwood tree thinking of her friend as if waiting for someone. One might want to say Linnea is put in the path of another certain jackrabbit perhaps by the hand of God or angels. One could even argue the fact it isn't just any rabbit that follows Linnea to this burial means this meeting is foretold. Perhaps there is a grand system of the cosmos that often puts the heartbroken within touch of a listening ear all over our globe. But saying so would mean we'd have to ignore the careful path this rabbit took in following the girl from Bunny's crime scene to her burial. One would need to ignore the rabbit's keen sense of things broken and unkind. And more importantly, we'd have to believe rabbits aren't astute creatures of justice and harbingers of vengeance.

Linnea is missing Bunny and her brother when she first sees the creature watching her. She doesn't flinch at the approaching jackalope, even when she sees the black and horned growths protruding from its head. Nor does she hope to avoid it. Instead, she looks upon the creature thoughtfully, and he upon her, and all the stories of little children meeting rabbits and creatures by chance become silly made-up things. The truth is jackrabbits believe in a graceful balance of good and evil. When they look to be things of fluff and sweetness, they are actually fast and shrewd. The trembling and twitching that is mistaken for fear is only a ruse, for when they do fight, they do so on their hind legs with quick jabs and the mobility of a feather-weight.

Linnea's brother and his rowdy friends had once told her stories of jackalopes and the games they play. But Linnea is never one to be teased or duped and as the town vet cleaned Bunny's ears and checked her nose, he answered her question and explained cottontail rabbits are susceptible to a certain virus that results in growths of keratin, the same things her hair and nails were made of, on their "little bunny heads" (which was his words, not hers). The vet may have told her to keep clear of such animals as they are infected with Shope papilloma at which point Linnea reasoned she wouldn't need to bother because a wild rabbit would never let her get that close to it unless it had its own motivations. And in this case it did.

Linnea doesn't even need to bother hearing the rabbit's version of what happened to Bunny. It's two-twitches of the nose is a signal to Linnea and as she begins describing the rowdy boys—the very ones that bullied her brother to swim far too long a distance across far too fast of a river—she can simply tell the rabbit knows the very ones. The ones with home-made slingshots who set empty cans along a busted fence for target practice. They'd bustle through the meadow thinking no can hear the howls and laughter. They'd talk of girls as bitches and when one would show a thinner skin, he'd immediately be pounced upon into a dog pile of insults and wrestling. After Brad died, these guilty boys were now quick to apologize and look away when they neared her screaming drunk father in town. Always ducking into some fake busy life when they saw her. Look at the phone. Look at this interesting piece of nothing on the sidewalk. Look at this thing on my hand, my skin because maybe in the lower layers of dermis there is an answer for the guilty. The rowdy boys: Brody, James, Jonas, and Christian. Killers of rabbits and brothers.

■

The camping trip was Brody's idea and while everyone knew they weren't going to where they were before when they lost their pack-member Brad, they all agreed on a place close enough. Close enough to not pretend it didn't happen, but not right there. Never right there. It is strange how none of them can last more than twenty minutes apart. When the body didn't resurface and there was nothing but the rush of water and the birds fussing over a new scent in the air, they had looked upon one another as strangers. No recognition of who they once were as if they'd been transported into a realm where iffy possibilities increased into probably's and certainly's and, finally, always. Always Brad didn't resurface on his own. Always the water rushed on. Always they were goaders of catastrophe. When each found himself alone, there was something in the body that revolted. An electric surge that came in jolts and pulses to the blood. Get out. Move. The cells screamed and refused to downshift. There was no settling anymore.

They hated one another and needed to see each other regularly in order to keep that hate alive. It is easier knowing one can hate himself as long as he is hated back. They shove the camping supplies around with a little more force than usual. They dump things on the ground with an added impact of frustration. They snap and bicker and as long as each of them feel the whip of another, they can continue putting up their campground, building a fire, and opening warm stolen beers. They talk, but no one says much. James is the first to think of mentioning Brad. Something funny he had said once. What was it? Another would have remembered the whole line. Someone else the context. But James and the others keep Brad stories and remember when's far from reach.

"I hate camping," James says, which isn't true but seems like the thing to say. The boys nod. The fire begins to smolder and the dozing off here and there turns into hefty snores. No one bothers to move into the tent, but instead they sleep on a hard ground that sucks up their heat.

James hears it first. Like a clearing of a throat or a muffled cough. It can't be Brad's because Brad is dead but it seems just like the often annoying tic he had right before suggesting something stupid or awful or too generous for a boy of fifteen. James pulls the sleeping bag over his head until he hears it again.

"Hey," Brody says almost to himself. Then again to the sleeping forms around him.

"Yeah. I heard it," James says.

Christian sits up abruptly when the noise gets louder. Jonas follows. It is more than a clearing of a throat now. There is a word or two in there. Too jumbled to hear, but so close. Close enough.

"Who's there?"

"Brody, shh!" James says. The voice seems to be coming from different places around them. It beckons. "Come here" or "Come" or "One". The others still can't make out the words, but know they won't be staying in their sleeping bags for long.

"Somebody fucking with us?" Jonas whispers.

"Get bent!" Brody yells. His voice falters at the end having tried on a voice he never had before.

"Bent?" James mouths.

A stirring, almost a foot step. Almost a repositioning or even a movement towards them.

"Get help." The voice says, which is enough for Jonas and Christian to forget about tying up their laces.

"I'm going to find out what the fuck is going on," Christian says. He smacks his flashlight twice against his palm and watches the beam slice through the air.

"Get that out of my face." James half-pretends to get outside of his sleeping bag. Brody has already begun working the bag down his legs, his feet finally shoving the thing in a clump nearer to the smoking logs of the fire.

"Help," the voice says.

Both Jonas and Christian take off. Quick at first to the edge of the camping area, but then slowly edging through the brush. James hears them for what seems like a few minutes before the shuffle of Brody getting his shoes on drowns out the area.

"I'm getting out of here."

"Don't leave us."

"Then hurry up. It's probably nothing anyway."

But James can't get himself up and to the truck. He can't imagine the drive along the dirt road without nightmaring something jumping out in front of them. He can never leave the woods fast enough. His body, a stone sinking.

As Brody's truck stalls twice on its way out of the campground, James finally stands up and starts towards the edge of the clearing.

∎

The jackalopes' horns are not unreal. In fact, the very scleroprotein that makes horns means "horn-like" in Greek. Keratin. We are not to forget the firm chain-like grip long scleroprotein filaments make when they reach across things soluble and active. They bond. A careful double coiling of rods locked together makes human hair and nails as well as parts of our own skin. In reptiles, birds, and amphibians keratin bundles make a tougher unmineralized tissue: the shell, scales, feathers, and beaks.

The horn-like growths on the rabbit are not easy or graceful in their development. It is of the same genetic make-up that offers our skin as
protection, which allows us to feel sensations and to regulate our own temperature. We live because of our skin organ and our skin exists because of keratin. But the reckless growth of hardened keratin tumors can take over the entire face of the rabbit infected with the Shope papilloma virus. Perhaps along the mouth, cheeks, and even the soft roll of dewlap.

Keratin doubles in length and strength each week. In that amount of time, human nails grow from 0.5 millimeters to 1.2 millimeters. The longest nails of a male recorded at 32 feet, 3.8 inches long. They more than coiled and twisted around themselves, they weighed the fingers and hands of the owner down causing chronic cramping and eventual disfigurement. A single strand of hair can potentially hold up to 100 grams. In theory, a whole head of hair could endure between 12,345-18,518 lbs. The acrobatic hair hangers are just a hint to this possibility. Keratin makes this so.

The protein is relentless and to James, it is deadly. When he first sees the jackalope, he imagines his face must look like that of Brad's father that day: shocked still. Carved into a moment of time forever. This small furry thing before him is the size and shape of the rabbit they had killed just yesterday. They pelted rocks at it with their newest slingshot and when they assumed it was dead, they rushed to its side. But it was still breathing, barely and in hard-earned huffs. Brody had been the one to put a larger rock to it. "Out of its misery," he had breathed. The boys felt relieved.

But the familiarity ends at the size and shape. The horns on the rabbit are uneven and crude. Not the elegant slope of an elk or pronghorn nor even the tidy, but impressive horns on the stuffed jackalopes in town. The rabbit boasts a tangle of hardened black prongs, at times looking more like mangled branches of a tree than antler. They gather along the top of the rabbit's head, with some near the mouth like tusks.

At first, James assumes the prickle under his skin is from nerve confusion, having learned he isn't in fact facing anything from a bobcat to a serial killer or even Brad's drunk and angry father in the woods taunting the boys to their death. Instead, it is an antlered-rabbit, once mythic or supernatural, but now just vulgar and diseased. And determined. Soon the prickle builds into a buzz of cellular activity. As the rabbit keeps its ground, its nose still the cute twitching thing of every childhood story, the keratin James' body houses extends its once sensible reach from one monomer to many. James trembles and begins to scratch at himself. The keratin doubling and tripling the filaments, filling itself up and pushing out the cellular filling and buffers into a cellular compost of types. He can feel it first in his nails. The growth of the nail so quick that the nailbed has no time to detach itself from the deadening nail. His skin raw and bleeding in pinpricks until the space of the nailbed is just too small and like a hangnail, it begins slicing its way into the sides of the fingers and then down each phalange. The nail extends almost inches now, almost half a foot, leaving a pulp of flesh and blood and dead cells where his hand used to be.

Where the skin doesn't tear as his fingernails and now toenails had, the water and fluids of his epidermis begin to flee their settled places. A slickness covers most of his arms and legs, chest neck and face, and soon the softer parts of his body: the belly, under his arms and the insides of his thighs, to his groin and rectum. Slick like a thin puss, almost just a heat rather than fluid. The water is pushed out by the work of keratin in his stratum spinosum, filament by filament it fills this lofty layer of his epidermis so there is no room but atop and below it. The hardening of the skin works both ways: a type of shell or scales building up and out of the skin and cutting down below into the subcutaneous level—snapping nerve receptors and glands along the way. Had he fingers left, he'd instinctively reach for his forearm hoping to both hold his keratin in and keep it from its new jagged reach to his bone.

Finally, it isn't the hair on top of his head that does him in. While the rest of the body spasms, dissected by its own protein spilling forth and in, the hair on his head grows as much as expected. Forcing its way through his scalp. The splotches of facial hair work into a new toughness and wind its way through its own forest of spiked tumors. While his entire body feels only of things gone rigid, like caked mud drying but from the inside out—it is the skin inside his nose that his body's shock will not ignore. The small hair follicles along the lateral nasal wall don't explode with the protective protein as the others have.

Instead it is like an unending flooding of keratin, a suffocation of the secretory cavity. Like the first quick seconds when Brad felt the water plow through his nose and throat. Like the first quick seconds Bunny scrounged around her lungs for air only to find an ooze escaping her. The follicles vibrate and twist around to hold in the keratin protein as it builds and builds. No bit of nature and men would force itself into James the same way Bunny and Brad had died, but instead it would plunge its way out of his skin. The jagged, robust horn-like tumors burst through his septum and skull, a tangle of strong-willed cells to destroy what weak a thing James turned out to be and to the defend the kinder things of this world.

BADLANDS SERENADE

Gerard Morrissette

"What is it that haunts the desolate Badlands near the place called Watch Dog Butte, South Dakota? There is a banshee loose in that region, a screeching nightmare in a long, tattered robe and disheveled hair that contorts its arms in strange gestures...The screams that issue forth from its mouth are said to have chilled the blood of those who have faced all manner of man and beast."

- Michael Norman and Beth Scott, *Haunted Heritage*

Alec adjusted his legs and steadied his sketchbook. He sat on a large rock roughly two miles off a trail in the badlands of South Dakota, part of a last cross country trip before he was due to start a new graphic design gig in Boston. With a future of staring at monitors before him, Alec planned to see and sketch as much as he could in the month he'd be on the road.

He didn't regret coming to the badlands—the banded canyons were beautiful, unlike anything he'd seen before. He just regretted the company.

Alec looked down from the canyon wall to his fellow campers—nine people he'd met in Deadwood the previous day. They were on spring break from a college he'd never heard of, and while they were only a bit younger than he, Alec felt a gulf of time and experience preventing him from liking these kids.

He absently doodled while watching Kara, the actual reason he was with them. He'd talked with her at a "saloon" in Deadwood, and shared a drink before she said she had to go meet her friends. She was his type—girl-next-door, nerdy, a nice smile and a sense of humor. She had asked if he wanted to join their trip into the Badlands and, feeling impetuous, he'd said yes. He'd felt anxious sitting next to Kara in her friend Phil's SUV, but in the hours it took their cars to make the drive from Deadwood there was humor and small talk to break the tension. While unloading the backpacks, Alec was concerned he wasn't seeing any water carried by the group—just a lot of alcohol. On the hike to find a campground he'd tried to casually bring up the lack of water. His concern was dismissed by the others—it was only one night, they said.

After that Alec was mostly quiet. He attempted to chat with Kara, but a kid named Jeremy had an obnoxious habit of interrupting by yelling out his own observations in sudden outbursts.

"Guys, look at that boulder! Totally sick colors, right?" Jeremy would say. He expressed a hundred variations of "This is so cool" while picking up objects along the way, and everybody else laughed along. Alec started trailing behind the others, stifling the desire to push Jeremy down a cliff.

The campsite was a corner in a shallow canyon, chosen because it would give Phil's guitar "good acoustics and shit." Alec didn't argue; he'd just dropped his pack and started to lay out his gear before noticing that he was the only one setting up. Everyone else was drinking, their packs tossed in a heap.

Alec decided he was being an ass. They were all friends; he shouldn't expect them to conform to his wishes. He joined the group to socialize a bit before lunch.

"Woooooooooo!" a yell echoed from below, shaking Alec from his thoughts. Kara and her friends didn't talk about much, but they all drank quickly and yelled "woo" at the top of their lungs to fill the moments between drinking and complaining about other students at school. This had led to Alec up to the rock he now occupied—but he saw now there was no longer enough light to draw scenery. He decided on figure sketches instead.

Quietly slipping to another rock, Alec looked towards Phil. Phil sat on a camping stool, a small collection of bottles strewn beneath him. He cradled his guitar in his lap, playing only the first thirty seconds of a song before shouting to one of the others, then moving on to a different tune. Alec didn't think Phil cared about music.

As Phil worked through the start of a Zeppelin song, Alec roughly outlined his posture. By the time he'd stopped playing to call for another drink, Alec was sharpening his pencil for detail work. He was suddenly aware of someone close to him, and looked to see Kara, her eyes glazed over from too much wine.

"I think I'm gonna throw up," Kara said, and covered her mouth with both hands.

"Are you okay?" Alec asked. He put a hand on her shoulder. She didn't answer, but instead stared toward Phil. Alec turned. Everyone over by the campfire was also staring. He looked to see what they were fixated on.

Several yards beyond Phil, a stranger had walked into the light of the campfire. Its feet crunched like that chalk on a driveway.

Alec slowly comprehended what he was seeing. A human skeleton had walked into camp.

The skeleton was bare except for leather scraps around its left ankle. Its bones were white and clean, though deeply cracked throughout the ribs and pelvis on the right side. With a flourish, its hand came up and lightly touched the brim of an imaginary hat. Its head bowed toward Phil.

Phil stumbled backwards, breaking the silence and scattering a few empty bottles in his wake. "No fucking way," he muttered.

Somewhere behind Alec one of the guys moaned miserably. Neither the skeleton nor Phil broke eye contact. It was impossible to read the skeleton's intent, while Phil was shaking and pale. Alec realized he was no longer sitting on the rock with his book, but rather standing with Kara.

Phil shuffled back a few steps as the skeleton suddenly stepped forward. It seated itself on Phil's stool, looked up at Phil, and then down at the guitar still clutched in his hand. Phil stared back, and swallowed. The skeleton repeated the head movement twice more. Phil did not react.

The skeleton quietly extended one index finger and pointed towards Phil. Phil whimpered. The finger moved down to the guitar. Phil looked at the instrument in his hands, blinked, and stared back at the skeleton.

The skeleton turned its hand palm up and closed its fingers twice in succession. The finger bones clacked like dominos being sorted.

Phil finally understood, and raised the guitar without moving any closer. The skeleton took it and laid it across its lap. Its skull moved back and forth, appraising the instrument, like a dog trying to understand a strange noise. In spite of himself, Alec giggled.

After a moment, the skeleton turned the guitar over in its hands, then settled into a playing position. Ten bony fingers began to pluck and flick along the strings in no apparent pattern. The canyon's acoustics amplified the discordance; Alex saw Kara's eyes begin to tear.

The skeleton suddenly stopped prodding and plucking, looked up at Phil, nodded once, and then looked back down to the guitar. Then it began to play.

It was hard for Alec to even tell that this was actually music. The skeleton played in a chaotic style, combining strums and slides, tapping on the body and using all five fingers of its right hand as picks to dance across the strings. At first the ugly sounds the finger bones made as they slid along the neck seemed to distract from the music, but soon these noises were incorporated into the combination of percussion and wildly ranging notes. Alec struggled to find an example of music to compare this to, but the closest he could manage was some chaotic child of Celtic and Spanish folk music, with a dash of delta blues. It was strange, beautiful and terrifying.

"In your face, Esteban," Kara croaked from her spot on the ground. Then she began to laugh. Alec frowned, but then saw it was the same with everyone. Drunks, at the point of panic moments ago, now swayed along with the music. Phil nodded his head in time with the skeleton's left foot as it tapped out the meter.

"He's good," Kara said next to Alec. "I could listen to him play all night."

"We don't even know it's a he," Alec muttered. As the skeleton played, the music took on warmth, even hopefulness. The others walked forward to get a better view of its hands as they blurred across the guitar.

"I think maybe we should—" Alec started to say to Kara, but he stopped speaking when he realized someone else had arrived.

Still keeping time, the skeleton was now looking over its shoulder as a figure descended down the rocky slope. It was a young woman, no older than her early twenties. Her dark hair was wild and flowed across her shoulders with a breeze that wasn't there. She wore a loose white gown with little detail. She moved in a crouch behind the skeleton, eyes fixed on it.

She seemed faded, like a low resolution image with color saturation reduced. Alec couldn't tell if her hair was red or black. It could have been either, depending on the light. Her eyes were large, full of awe as she listened to the skeleton play.

"She's pretty," Kara said as she swayed next to Alec. She wrapped her arm around his waist and leaned her head on his shoulder in a comfortable way.

"Pretty? Sure. But not right," he said, fumbling to explain his unease.

The woman knelt by the skeleton, her gown pooled around her as she looked on with adoration. She didn't blink, and as the music gathered speed and complexity, she fidgeted and scurried back and forth, anticipating some important outcome.

Empty eyes gazing back at the woman, the skeleton finished playing with a rapid escalation of notes and flourishes. Then it spun the guitar so that it was presented in outstretched hands towards Phil, who simply stared back with a dumb grin on his face.

"You got this, dude!" Jeremy yelled at Phil from just a few paces away. Phil flinched and stepped forward, taking the guitar. As he retrieved a pick from his pocket, Alec saw both the woman and skeleton lean forward.

"I think we need to get moving," Alec whispered to Kara as he stepped back. He put one foot on the rocks, still holding her hand.

"I want to hear Phil play first," she said, and let his hand go.

Alec stepped up onto the rocks and tried to think of something to motivate Kara. Then Phil started playing.

Looking comfortable, Phil breezed through the first 20 notes or so from a Creedence tune before he screwed up a chord. "Oops," he said with a smile as he went to start over, looking up at his audience.

The skeleton's head drooped suddenly, and then rotated until it locked eyes with the woman. A look of deep sorrow cascaded across her features. As she turned to look upon Phil, the skeleton crumbled from the stool, scattering bones on the canyon floor.

"Oh, dude," Phil began, but he was cut off as the woman lurched to her feet and screamed.

Alec felt as though he'd been punched in the kidneys. He found himself lying on his back near a prone and shaking Kara. Turning his head, a wave of nausea made him groan, and he struggled to focus his eyes. A stream of saliva ran from his mouth.

Alec saw Jeremy stumbling, his arms flailing as he struggled to stay upright. Jeremy's chest and face was covered in a thick layer of clumped tissue, torn cloth and blood. Several long pieces of thin wood protruded from his abdomen. Jeremy tumbled forward on his stomach, driving the wood deeper into his body in ragged splinters. He convulsed a few times, but then stopped moving.

As Alec forced himself to rise, he couldn't see Phil anywhere—just blood and cloth and meat sprayed all over the campsite. He yelled for Kara to get up, and found that he could barely hear his own voice over the ringing in his ears.

The woman was standing tall, shoulders back, rigid in her posture. Her eyes scanned across the campers. With a heaving motion, she grimaced and began to draw air deep into her lungs.

Alec squatted, grabbed Kara by her belt and began pulling her up. He scrambled awkwardly toward the shallow wall of the canyon, dragging her flailing body behind him. She'd suffered greater injuries than he had, and the alcohol was making it tougher for her to collect herself. He tried to secure a better hold on her, risking a glance at the woman as he did.

As Alec turned, the woman released her breath. This time it was no sudden burst of noise, but a controlled expression of malevolent sound.

A young girl named Shonda dropped to her knees, her mouth open in a scream that was drowned out. She pressed her hands tightly over her eyes. As Alex watched, her body shuddered and her hands fell from her face, revealing the ruined craters of her eye sockets. She collapsed forward into the dirt, her body vibrating from the woman's scream.

Feeling as though a dozen jackhammers were loose inside his flesh, Alec heaved Kara up onto a rock. She began vomiting, the slick mucus making her harder to grasp. Alec heard the sound of his own loud whimpering. The woman had not turned towards them yet. He knew they were alive only as long as it stayed that way.

With Kara secured on the stone, Alec clambered up the rocks and lay on his belly on top of the canyon wall. He rotated around to reach for Kara, and tried to rub sand from his left eye but only managed more irritation with his bile-covered hand.

The woman had advanced on a camper whose name Alec did not know. The man had crawled up into a narrow crevice that fissured off from the main camp site. As the woman bellowed, Alec saw the man's flesh undulating like ocean waves as the crevice channeled the sound waves on all sides. His confused expression never betrayed awareness of what was happening, until his whole body burst like a ripe melon and showered onto the rocks below.

With a cough, the woman ceased screaming. Alec reached down and grabbed Kara's arm. He braced his legs and heaved, dragging her up out of the canyon. Then he reached down to grab her jeans for leverage, and glanced over her shoulder.

The woman stood below them, looking up. Her spine arched as she pulled in a ragged breath. "No no no," Alec shouted, hauling on Kara with his back and legs.

A sound like a freight train washed over Alec, hurling him away from the ledge and across a dozen yards of stony ground. An agonizing burst in his head cut the noise short as his body crashed, forcing the air from him.

Alec found himself prone near a slope down into the canyon. He tried to prop himself up on an elbow, but his left arm didn't respond. Alec couldn't focus enough to tell if he still had a left arm at all. The angle made it impossible to look.

He brought his right hand before his eyes. A great tangle of long brown hair connected to a pulpy mass of tissue was entwined in his fingers.

Alec dropped his hand and fell into a fit of hitching, painful sobs. He could feel a fluttering in his chest, like a wet flag in a strong wind. As he cleared his throat to call for help, Alec realized he was also stone deaf.

He lay still, hoping he would feel the vibrations in the ground if the woman walked up behind him. He tried to focus on nothing, so that a distraction wouldn't prevent him from sensing her footsteps.

Down In the canyon, Alec saw the skeleton stroll into view from the trail that led to the campsite. It appeared to be plucking at loose strings on the broken neck of Phil's guitar. Not far behind came the woman, hands clutched to her chest as she dutifully followed her minstrel.

Alec was still watching them walk off into the darkness when his eyes began to lose focus. Soon it was as dark as it was quiet.

WORDS OF TERROR

ADRIAN VAN YOUNG is the author of *The Man Who Noticed Everything* (Black Lawrence Press), and *Shadows in Summerland*, forthcoming from ChiZine Publications. His work has been published or is forthcoming in *Black Warrior Review*, *VICE*, and *Slate*. He lives in New Orleans with his wife Darcy and son Sebastian.

DANIELLE RENINO is a ghost enthusiast and aspiring young adult author. She has a minor in creative writing and a passion for abandoned asylum photography. Her two favorite things are words and rot.

STEPHEN T. BROPHY writes words for fun and money. His novella *The Villain's Sidekick* and its prequel *The Eternity Conundrum* can be found co-existing peacefully in their natural habitat at Budget Press. They are priced to move.

AMBER SPARKS is the author of *May We Shed These Human Bodies*, and co-author (with Robert Kloss and illustrator Matt Kish) of *The Desert Places*. Her second story collection, *The Unfinished World and Other Stories*, will be published by Liveright/Norton in 2016. She can be found @ambernoelle, or at *ambernoellesparks.com*

LIZZ HUERTA is a poet, fiction writer, and essayist. She paints wrought iron to pay the bills. She is currently working on a young adult novel.

THOMAS MARTIN works on the river and drinks canned Yuenglings. His writing has been featured in Kyler Martz's *Nightswimmer* and a few issues of *The Radvocate*.

STEVE JONES grew up in a small Maine town and attended the University of Maine. He now lives in Massachusetts, but still visits that small Maine town when he can. Steve's work has been featured in the *ZombieBomb!* anthology. Steve enjoys being outside with his family.

ZACK WENTZ's work has appeared, or is forthcoming, in *James Gunn's Ad Astra*, *New York Tyrant*, *[PANK]*, *Black Clock*, *Weird Tales*, *decomP*, *NANO Fiction*, *3: AM*, *Fiction International*, *Word Riot*, and elsewhere. He runs *New Dead Families*. *newdeadfamilies.com*

KIRSTEN ALENE is the author of *Japan Conquers the Galaxy* (2013), *Unicorn Battle Squad* (2012) and the novella *Love in the Time of Dinosaurs* (2010). Her work has been published in *The Magazine of Bizarro Fiction*, *Innsmouth Magazine*, *New Dead Families*, *Small Doggies Magazine*, *The Battered Suitcase*, *Ellipsis*, and *Rivets*.

CAMERON PIERCE is the Wonderland Book Award-winning author of *Our Love Will Go the Way of the Salmon* and other books. He is also the head editor of Lazy Fascist Press. He lives in Astoria, Oregon with his wife and daughter.

JS BREUKELAAR is the author of *American Monster* and *Ink*. Her work has appeared in *Juked, Fantasy Magazine, Prick of the Spindle, Opium, New Dead Families, Go(b)bet Magazine*, and elsewhere. She lives in Sydney, San Diego, New York… and elsewhere, but you can almost always find her at *thelivingsuitcase.com*.

HEATHER FOWLER is a poet, fiction writer, essayist, and novelist. She is the author of the story collections *Suspended Heart, People with Holes, This Time, While We're Awake*, and *Elegantly Naked In My Sexy Mental Illness,* and she is Poetry Editor at *Corium Magazine*. Visit her at *heatherfowler.com*

MEG TUITE is author of two story collections, *Bound By Blue* and *Domestic Apparition*. Her collection *Bare Bulbs Swinging* won the Twin Antlers Poetry award. She teaches at Santa Fe Community College, is editor for *Santa Fe Literary Review* and Connotation Press, and has a column at JMWW. *megtuite.com*

BRIAN KRANS is a native of Wisconsin Rapids, and is a lifelong cheesehead. Now living in Oakland, CA, he's a journalist, author, and host of *The Rock Town Podcast*. He has a dog named Friday.

BEN SEGAL is the author of *Pool Party Trap Loop* and *78 Stories*, co-author of *The Wes Letters*, and co-editor of *The Official Catalog of the Library of Potential Literature*. His fiction has been published by *Tin House, Tarpaulin Sky, Puerto del Sol*, and *The Collagist*. He lives in Los Angeles.

JAMIE GREFE is the author of the *DECKER: CLASSIFIED* novelization (with Tim Heidecker and Gregg Turkington), *Domo ArigaDIE!!!* (Rooster Republic Press), *The Mondo Vixen Massacre* (Eraserhead Press) and more. He has written for the screen and is currently an MFA in Creative Writing student at New England College.

NATANYA ANN PULLEY is an Assistant Professor at the University of South Dakota and the Fiction Editor at South Dakota Review. She has a PhD in Fiction Writing from the University of Utah. Natanya's publications include *Western Humanities Review, AS/US journal for indigenous women, The Collagist*, and *McSweeney's Open Letters*.

GERARD MORRISSETTE is a Masshole who now lives in the Omaha metro region. His work has appeared in comics from Terminal Press. He likes old school practical effects in horror, makes a mean chili, and some people know him as the Infinity Gauntlet of Pork.

BEN LOORY is the author of *Stories for Nighttime and Some for the Day* (Penguin, 2011), and *The Baseball Player and the Walrus* (Dial Books for Young Readers, 2015). His tales have been published in *The New Yorker*, been heard on *This American Life*, and performed in Los Angeles and London.

ART OF TERROR

ADAM MILLER is a gallery director and professional art guy. Clients include Budweiser, Nuclear Blast Records and Montserrat College of Art. His work has received recognition from G4TV, The New York Times, *Fangoria* and MSNBC. He writes, teaches, speaks, paints and photographs his way through the art world. *facebook.com/millerstrations*

HAIG DEMARJIAN's work spans many media. In addition to painting, printmaking and drawing he also co-masterminded the award-winning film *Die You Zombie Bastards!* He writes and draws his comic book *Super Inga*, available at *SuperIngaSaga.com*. He's a Professor of Art + Design at Salem State University. See more at *artofHaig.com*.

PAT KELLEY is a loner and a rebel. He likes gummy worms. *pattkelley.com*

DOMINIC VIVONA is a Pennsylvanian illustrator and contributor to the *New York Times* bestselling graphic novel, *FUBAR*. He is an award-winning artist and animator whose work has been recognized by the Philadelphia Independent Film Festival and the Platinum Comic Book Challenge. Mostly, he just likes drawing warriors and barbarians. *D.vivona1@gmail.com*

BEN DONAHUE resides in the darkness outside Lowell, MA. He can be found illustrating his dark fantasy *The Mearyan Seal* and the V.S. Holmes' *Reforged* series. He loves gritty concept art, illustration, and portraits with pastel, charcoal, and digital media. Ben graduated Montserrat College of Art in 2012. *bendonahueart.com*

NICKOLAI KILIN is a self-taught artist currently residing in Central Florida. Originally from College Park, Maryland, he is a lover of all things art and pop culture. Most recently, he has developed a passion for tattoos and is working through his tattoo apprenticeship in the heart of the sunshine state. *CtrlAltCassie@gmail.com*

ENZO GARZA has created work for bands (Moonmen From Mars), comic series (*A Comic Book*) and pulp (*States of Terror*). He recently curated the *Boss Krang* art exhibit for ACME Superstore, and is currently self-publishing *Sensation BOOM*. He also participates in the comic book fight club MAZZATE. *enzogarza.com*

ZACK ATKINSON, born in Brasil, grew up in Maine, resides in NY and works as an art director at Universal Music Group. Makes bad decisions, rides a bicycle, lacks the ability to shave and only 2 cubes with bourbon. Makes things with other things. Feel free to bother him at *zackatkinson.com*.

HEATHER SCOGGINS is an award-winning illustrator living in Salem, Massachusetts and specializes in painting with gouache. Other interests include fitness, ferrets, and video games. *heatherscoggins.com*

DANIEL KERN is an illustrator and visual artist based in southern Massachusetts. He lives with his two cats and a few ghosts. He drinks too much coffee and will most likely be buried in a good book when he should be working. Instagram: @danielkernart

DAVID FERREIRA is an award-winning illustrator working for clients in the advertising, publishing and editorial markets. David has recently created illustrations for Unilever, Hasbro, BacardiUSA, Heineken and ESPN. David is also a passionate teacher, and instructs illustration, painting and drawing courses for colleges, museums and art organizations throughout New England.

SAM J ROYALE is an Earth-based illustrator and animator who eats cookies, draws and paints pictures, and makes cartoons like *Cardboard Paper*. Contact him through *samjroyale.com* to see if he is available for freelance work or commissions.

CRAIG SCHAFFER is an award-winning visual journalist who works in the newspaper industry where he creates two weekly visual columns; *Snapshot* and *Sketchbook*. His published works include courtroom drawings, comics, infographics, and natural science illustrations. He lives with his family in Sinking Spring, PA. *craig-schaffer.com*

RICH WOODALL is a New Hampshire-based artist and writer, best known for his creator-owned titles *Johnny Raygun, ZombieBomb!* and *Kyrra Alien Jungle Girl* (with artist Craig Rousseau). His work has appeared in IDW, Dark Horse, and Image Comics, among others. He loves tacos, cheeseburgers, cake and Thor. *johnraygun.deviantart.com*

HANNA TAWATER completed her MFA in Writing at UCSD in 2014. Her poetry and prose can be found online and in print, including in *States of Terror 1*. She contributed an illustration to this volume, since the editors wouldn't let her write another story. She currently lives in San Diego.

KARL SLOMINSKI began drawing comics as soon as his tiny, claw-like hand could grasp a pen. Fueled by black coffee and rock n' roll, he spirals down the rabbit hole of comics as the artist of *Golgotha, Run Like Hell*, and *Ashes: A Firefighter's Tale*. He loves you very much. *slomotionart.net*

ZACHARY NAYLOR graduated from Montserrat College of Art in 2015 with a BFA in Printmaking, and currently lives and works in the greater Boston area. His practices include etchings and drawings that focus on the fallibility of the human mind, reacting to societal norms and behaviors. *zachary-naylor.squarespace.com*

JB ROE is a Chicago-based artist and illustrator originally from Lakeland, Florida. Upcoming work will be featured in books from both Black Mask Studios and Image Comics. He loves professional wrestling and is terrible at writing bios. *jbroe.com*

TOM TORREY has a BFA in illustration, and has spent many years trying to shake the scars of a formal art education and live the life of an outsider artist. Best known as the "Robot Guy," he sculpts robots out of found objects and lets them loose on the world. *robotswebe.tumblr.com*

FRANK CASAZZA has dedicated his life to the world of Eyeformation. An imaginative, child-like sense of character is visible in all of his work. His illustrations have been featured in a variety of publications. He has generated an international audience and clientele in China, Belgium, Italy and the UK. *eyeformation.net*

GEOFF MOSSE is a humble, hardworking freelance writer and artist that lives in a heavily armed and fortified compound where he is constantly producing work for various media. His latest graphic novel *The Mick* is available from Red Handed Studios.

JOE HALEY's drawings have an average lifespan of roughly seventeen seconds. His entry into this anthology survived long enough to be scanned, after which it escaped and is still at large. His comic series, *The Underburbs*, also exists somewhere. *underburbs.deviantart.com*

JOSH MORRISSETTE is a photo-based illustrator from central Massachusetts. He is one part Jedi, one part Sith, and spends his days teaching his child about the perks of the dark side. His work has been exhibited throughout New England and in several publications. *facebook.com/jomoillphoto*, *@JMIphoto*

RESEARCH OF TERROR

Barber, Sally. <u>Myths and Mysteries of Michigan: True Stories of the Unsolved and the Unexplained.</u> Rowman & Littlefield, 2011.

Bunker, Melissa. <u>Hooo... Yeah Boy! Fictional and Factional Funnies Of North Carolina</u>. Lulu.com Press.

Campbell, Susan et al. <u>Connecticut Curiosities: Quirky Characters, Roadside Oddities & Other Offbeat Stuff</u>. Rowman & Littlefield, 2010.

Carlson, Charlie. <u>Weird Florida: Your Travel Guide to Florida's Local Legends and Best Kept Secrets</u>. Sterling Publishing Company Inc., 2009.

Cline, Bruce. <u>More History, Mystery, and Hauntings of Southern Illinois</u>. Black Oak Media Inc., 2012.

Francis, Scott. <u>Monster Spotter's Guide to North America</u>. F+W Media, 2007.

Gerhard, Ken. <u>Encounters with Flying Humanoids: Mothman, Manbirds, Gargoyles and other Winged Beasts</u>. Llewellyn Worldwide, 2013.

Godfrey, Linda S. <u>Monsters of Wisconsin: Mysterious Creatures in the Badger State</u>. Stackpole Books, 2011.

Godfrey, Linda S. <u>Real Wolfmen: True Encounters in Modern America</u>. Penguin, 2012.

Hancock, David M. <u>Jackalope Hunting</u>. David Hancock, 2004.

Lankford, Andrea. <u>Haunted Hikes: Spine-tingling Tales and Trails From North America's National Parks</u>. Santa Monica Press, 2006.

McNamee, Thomas. <u>The Killing of Wolf Number Ten: The True Story</u>. Easton Studio Press LLC, 2014.

Newton, Michael. <u>Hidden Animals: A Field Guide to Batsquatch, Chupacabra, and Other Elusive Creatures</u>. ABC-CLIO, 2009.

Norman, Michael & Beth Scott. <u>Haunted Heritage: A Definitive Collection of North American Ghost Stories</u>. Macmillian, 2007.

Richards, Sally. Personal interview. May 2015.

Roberts, Paul Dale et al. <u>H.P.I. Chronicles, Volume 1</u>. Lulu.com Press. 2011.

Rux, Bruce. <u>Architects of the Underworld: Unriddling Atlantis, Anomalies of Mars and the Mystery of the Sphinx</u>. Frog Books, 1996.

Salcedo-Chourré, Tracy. <u>Best Hikes Near Reno and Lake Tahoe</u>. Globe Pequot, 2014.

Sillery, Barbara. <u>The Haunting of Louisiana</u>. Pelican Publishing, 2001.

AFTERWORD

We hope you've enjoyed our second weird trek through the union. We know we've learned a whole lot more about the uncanny oogie-boogies that share this land with us.

You may have noticed a few discrepancies in our sophomore collection. The first volume contained a California story already, didn't it? So why another one here— and in San Diego, no less? Well, we appreciate your indulgence. We couldn't pass up the opportunity to feature a beastie found right in our own backyard. Would you?

After completing the first book, we resolved to make each collection better than the last. Stick around with us for the final volume and you'll see a few more twists and turns, a few more unconventional detours. What we hope to capture in these tales is the bizarre, unpredictable nature of our varied nation, encapsulated by monster stories trawled from our collective id.

Our terrifying tour of America is nearly over. We hope you'll go with us all the way. Don't worry, gas is on us. Or, if you want, we can let you out at this stop. But first, ask yourself: after all you've seen so far, don't you want to know what's left?

We certainly do. We've got a full tank, a bag of Halloween candy, and an empty seat in the back. See you on the road.

—M.L. & K.M.